**Westminster**
*Gracious Retirement Living*

# Daffodils at High Meadows

*For the library at Westminster —*
*Elizabeth Buttenheim*

# Daffodils at High Meadows

## and Other Stories

### Elizabeth Buttenheim

iUniverse, Inc.
New York Lincoln Shanghai

**Daffodils at High Meadows**
*and Other Stories*

Copyright © 2005 by Elizabeth Buttenheim

All rights reserved. No part of this book may be used or reproduced by any means, graphic, electronic, or mechanical, including photocopying, recording, taping or by any information storage retrieval system without the written permission of the publisher except in the case of brief quotations embodied in critical articles and reviews.

iUniverse books may be ordered through booksellers or by contacting:

iUniverse
2021 Pine Lake Road, Suite 100
Lincoln, NE 68512
www.iuniverse.com
1-800-Authors (1-800-288-4677)

ISBN-13: 978-0-595-37378-9 (pbk)
ISBN-13: 978-0-595-81775-7 (ebk)
ISBN-10: 0-595-37378-X (pbk)
ISBN-10: 0-595-81775-0 (ebk)

Printed in the United States of America

*For Geg, whose love and encouragement and support have been a constant in my life for almost sixty years.*

# Contents

High Meadows ........................................................................... 1
Felicity and George .................................................................... 6
Sophie and Andrew .................................................................. 19
The Dunham Sisters ................................................................. 28
Katherine and Charlie .............................................................. 39
Barbara and Tom ..................................................................... 54
Flower Power .......................................................................... 72

## Other Stories

Last Leave ............................................................................... 85
Roman Epiphany ..................................................................... 95
Mary, Mary ............................................................................ 107
The Birthday Party ................................................................. 126
A Butterfly for my Cocoon ..................................................... 145

# High Meadows

High Meadows is a retirement community in a college town in western Massachusetts. The property on which it is built was once a dairy farm on the outskirts of the town, and like most farms in this part of New England, it was mostly composed of pastures on the sides of gently, and sometimes not so gently, sloping hillsides. In summer they were verdant and richly rimmed with wild flowers that grew just outside low stone walls confining the cattle that grazed there. In winter they were usually covered with snow and crisscrossed with the tracks of cross country skiers, students from the college who had an arrangement with the farmer that allowed them to ski there.

The college had an informal agreement with the farmer that when he or his heirs wished to sell the property, the college would have the right of first refusal. But twenty years ago, when a grandson of the farmer was turned down for admission, his grandfather abruptly sold the land to a developer of retirement communities. The developer believed that alumni of the college were good prospective customers, and that others, not alumni, would be drawn to this charming New England college town to retire. He was correct, and the units sold quickly. Now there is a waiting list of prospective buyers, and the current residents are rather smug about their foresight in buying into the community early.

There are about three hundred and fifty people living here now, and they are an interesting and varied group. Several are retired professors from the local college and also from other well known colleges and universities. Some of these have national reputations, at least among academicians. One is a Nobel Prize winner in the field of physics. No one at High Meadows, except for one other retired physics professor, understands much about his award winning work, but all the residents are proud of his presence among them and point him out to their visitors. His being there gives the place a certain cachet.

There are two past college presidents and two former CEOs of Fortune 500 companies, and a number of retired high level corporate executives. For some of these, relinquishing the steering wheel has been hard. But these former leaders are useful citizens of High Meadows, for they are only too happy to become chairmen of the committees that run the community. If they tend to turn their committees into something resembling a General Motors Board of Directors just to decide whether the windows should be washed once or twice a year, well, there are other residents who are delighted that someone is saving them from these responsibilities.

Not surprisingly there are more women than men in the community, and many of these are widows of accomplished men. The population of High Meadows is too old (the average age is seventy-nine) for most of the women residents to have benefited from the feminist movement of the late twentieth century, but a few of the most recent arrivals have had successful careers. One of the former college presidents is a woman. There is a woman physician, a writer of children's books, and a former ballet dancer. There are also women whose work has been at the highest level of volunteerism: past national presidents of The Garden Club of America and the League of Women Voters and several trustees of colleges, some still serving.

As would be expected of such a group of bright lights (although, alas, some bulbs have dimmed), the interests and activities of the residents are broad and often intellectual. Dinner conversations range from political and social issues to the arts and the latest books. There is also a considerable amount of gossip about the daily affairs of the community and its residents. Whatever the topic, the dialogue is lively.

Most people find the setting of the community and its gray clapboard buildings quite attractive. Midway up a hillside, previously the site of the old farmhouse, is a rambling multi-storied facility. This south-facing building contains the public rooms and staff offices of High Meadows, as well as all the apartments for the residents. Around it, a number of small cottages have replaced the barns and other outbuildings of the farm. The cottages were the first units to be sold, in spite of the inclement winters and the difficulty of walking to the main building for meals. Most of the residents at High Meadows are intrepid New Englanders and are not daunted by seasonal ice and snow. Those who are spend the winter months in Florida.

In a large open area at the center of the property is a small pond created by the farmer for his diary cows. It is surrounded by poplar trees that provided shade for the cows in the heat of summer. Around the perimeter of this former pasture is a crumbling stone wall, and just within the wall is a walking path that is widely used by the residents. Along the path are occasional benches where walkers can sit and rest. The pasture, which was previously well grazed by cattle, is now mowed about twice a summer to keep it from reverting to woods. It is no longer a pasture but a meadow where abundant wild flowers bloom.

Enough time has passed since High Meadows was built for the new landscaping to mature. There are trees and shrubs and gardens around the main building. A greenhouse behind it is surrounded by garden plots that the residents use to raise flowers and vegetables in the summer.

Almost all the residents at High Meadows like their new home. "How lucky we are to be here" is a refrain often heard in the dining room at night. Their homes, whether cottages or apartments, are smaller than their former ones, but, as the residents have grown older, smallness has come to seem an asset rather than a liability. "So much easier to take care of," they say, "so many possessions disposed of, so much less clutter." They feel liberated—from ownership, from responsibility, from all the cares of maintaining a home and property. At a time when many of their old friends are dying, they are making new ones. They are, they say, free to do things they have always wanted to do. "At last," they tell each other, "I have time to paint—to write my memoirs—to travel—to improve my French—to organize our photographs—to take up the piano again…" And some of them do these things.

But many do not. Some make a desultory start and then give up. And strangely, they make the same excuses they made before they came to High Meadows. "It would take too much time—I don't know where to begin—I'll never need to speak French again—my fingers are too stiff to play well." And so on. The truth is, it is sometimes enough for them to know these possibilities exist, that their lives are still open ended, that there are opportunities they could pursue if they chose. "Maybe next year," they tell themselves.

All of them recognize that this is the final stage of their lives. They understand that many old dreams will never be more than dreams: the cabin in Montana (too far from their doctors); the trip to see the Great Wall of China (too many steps for their arthritic knees); a last run down their favorite ski slope (too dangerous for their weakened bones). They know that what lies ahead is mostly loss; loss of health, of strength, of beauty, of memory, loss of a beloved spouse, and finally loss of life itself. Yet in the face of these inevitabilities, they live mostly with courage and often with grace. It helps to be together with others who are experiencing the same indignities of old age. They see that nothing is more valued here than a brave face and a sense of humor and a strong will in the face of adversity, and for their own sakes and the sake of others, these are the attributes they cultivate as they live out the last years of their lives together.

# Felicity and George

Felicity Todd sits in a chair on the tiny balcony of her apartment. It is a hot day, the end of August, and she is wearing a thin cotton caftan. Sitting as she often does out here, with her legs folded under her, she resembles a small, round Buddha, frozen in meditation, at peace with the world. But Felicity is not meditating, nor is she at peace; she is suffering great pain and feeling terrible rage, and her emotions have turned her to stone.

She and her husband George have spent the morning with an oncologist. He has told them, with the usual impersonality that masks the distress he always feels on such occasions, that George's cancer has returned. Even though they have suspected this might be so, it is not true until Dr. Craig says it is. He knows his words are dashing all their hopes, but there are decisions to be made, and he believes they must have all the information they need to make those decisions.

"It's spread more than I would have expected," he tells them. "It's in both lungs, and the lymph nodes indicate it's spread elsewhere as well. I'm surprised you haven't had more symptoms." (He means more pain.) "We can't cure it, you know, but we can get you more time, and when it gets bad, we can see that you're kept comfortable. You responded very well to the chemotherapy before. No reason to think you won't again."

But George remembers all too well how he responded to the treatments five years ago. Yes, they drove the cancer into remissiom, but at a cost. They made him sicker than he had ever been in his life. He vomited so much that he began to wonder if the chemotherapy was intended to make him vomit up the cancer itself. Sometimes he actually looked in the toilet to see if it was there, some great gory ball of cells. Yet the treatments had given him five more years, important years, in which he had spent a summer in France, gotten closer to his children, been blessed with another grandchild, and learned to dance the tango. He would go through chemotherapy again for five more good years.

But then Dr. Craig is saying, "Of course, you won't have the same results as before. It's too far gone this time."

"So what are we talking about, in time, I mean, Dr. Craig?"

"Well, you know, these things aren't totally predictable. I'd guess, and it's only a guess, you understand." Dr. Craig hates to be pinned down—he's been wrong before, and sometimes by a lot. "I'd guess maybe six or eight months with treatment, three or four without."

"Then that settles that. I'm not going through that hell again just to get two or three extra months."

Dr. Craig presses as hard as he dares, although knowing what lies ahead, he would make the same choice as George.

"There have been some improvements in the last five years, George, better pain control, for instance. We might even be able to get you some marijuana. It's not legal, of course, but it's available, and I've seen it help a lot of patients on chemotherapy."

George hesitates for only a moment. Felicity holds her breath, but then he says, "Nope, not for me," and she knows there will be no changing his mind.

Most of the rest of the visit is with a nurse who explains George's medication routine and the diet he is to follow. Felicity listens, but nothing makes sense to her. Her brain refuses to process the information. What the nurse is saying doesn't matter, she thinks. It can't possibly be true. The doctor has confused George's tests with someone else's. It isn't until they are leaving and the nurse presses a pamphlet on the local hospice system into her hand that she begins to realize all that lies ahead for them.

In the car they say little of what they have just heard. A thousand practicalities flood George's mind. There are so many loose ends to tie up, he thinks: my will and Filly's to check with our lawyer, that education trust to set up for the grandchildren, my stamp collection—who will want it, if anybody? Our symphony subscription, should we turn it in or offer it to someone at Meadows? I'll need to cancel the winter rental in Florida and our auto-train tickets. It is easier for him to think of these matters that require action than of the cancer that is growing inside him.

Felicity sits beside him thinking her own thoughts. She wonders how to tell the children. She thinks it will be better for her to phone them when he's not at home. She will cry and they will cry—oh, it will certainly be very hard. Maybe she should write them a carefully thought out letter. Then they can call him after they have had a chance to pull themselves together. Should the grandchildren be told, not the young ones, of course, but the others? She decides she will leave that to their parents. And how about George's sister? And his cousin Henry, who is also his best friend? Should she tell them or should he?

They are both sunk in their own thoughts all the way home. When they are back at the apartment, she fixes a salad for their lunch—he is especially fond of salads—and when they finish eating, he says he is tired and wants to lie down awhile. In the bedroom, he takes off his shoes and tie and then his trousers which he carefully hangs in his closet. He has always been a neat and fastidious man. Felicity likes to brag that she has never had to pick up after him. He folds the bed spread to the foot of the bed and lies down, covering himself with a thin handmade quilt. He thinks his mind is spinning too much for him to sleep, but in a few minutes he dozes off.

So now Felicity is sitting on the terrace trying to plan ahead, but she is too miserable and too angry to think clearly. It wasn't like this the other time, she says to herself. Dr. Craig told us then that Toddy's chances were good for recovery, and he was right. Bad as those treatments were, he got better. I thought he was cured. It's cruel to have been tricked and now to be offered no hope at all. She directs her anger at Fate and at Dr. Craig, but also at her husband.

How could he let this happen, she thinks, unreasonably. How could he not know he was sick earlier when treatment would still have worked? How can he leave me when he knows he is the center of my existence? And how can I live without him, my love, my life? She bites on the knuckle of her thumb and moans. It is more than she can bear.

They have been married for forty-eight years, and now she knows they will never make the fiftieth anniversary that they have been planning since their forty-fifth. They wanted to include all their children and grandchildren. A rented house in Provence, a cottage in England, a stay at a ranch in Montana, so many possibilities, and after this morning's news, no possibilities at all. Part of the fun was in the planning, and now she knows they will never mention their fiftieth again. "Oh, how sad, how sad," she whispers, and feels shamed by her self-pity, for she recognizes the emotion for what it is. It is a flaw in her nature that she has never overcome. She understands that at this time all her concerns should be for her husband, for he is the one after all who has heard his death sentence with no appeal from Dr. Craig, a trusted friend.

But Dr. Craig has also offered him more time with new treatments, and he has turned that offer down, and that is the root of her anger. For surely he knows, he must know, that she would bear anything, anything, for a few more weeks or months, even days, of his presence. She would even bear seeing him suffer, which would be more painful than suffering herself. But he didn't give her a voice in his decision. He blurted out his refusal to accept treatment without giving her a chance to say a word. She wanted to beg him not to leave her, to stay with her for as long as he can at any price, but she knows at some deeper level than her desire for him to stay that this decision is his to make.

They have had a charmed life together. Their older daughter, Molly, who has been through a painful divorce, has told them many times how lucky they are in their marriage, and Felicity agrees completely. Just finding each other involved luck. They had been in the right place at the right time, that is, the freshman class at Boston College where they sat side by side in a mandatory English class that bored her because it was not challenging enough, and him because he had little interest in literature. He was a tall, popular boy from a Philadelphia suburb, a graduate of a well known prep school. She was a short, shy girl from a public high school in Cambridge who was just beginning to come into her own. Because he found her enchanting, his friends assumed she must be. They were inseparable throughout their college years and were married three days after they graduated.

There have been misfortunes in their life together, even tragedies: a stillborn baby son; a younger brother of Felicity's killed in Korea; Molly's unhappy marriage. But their love for their children and each other, all their shared interests, and yes, thinks Felicity, even the painful times, have bound them together. She thinks of the clumps of daylilies she divides, their roots so intertwined that she needs two garden forks and all her strength to tear them apart, destroying many of them in the process. Her roots and George's, the hidden part of the long, loving relationship that nourishes them both, are about to be torn apart, and surely a part of her will be destroyed when they are.

She needs the comfort of being close to him. She goes into their bedroom and crawls across the bed where he is lying and presses herself against his back. She puts her arm over him and her hand on his chest and is reassured by this contact and by his slow quiet breathing. He wakes just enough to place his hand over hers and then sleeps again. She lies very still while tears gather in her eyes and roll down her face.

Not a sound of her weeping escapes her but in a minute he wakes again, and this time he speaks.

"Don't cry, Filly, please don't cry."

Now that he is awake, she begins to sob aloud. He turns on his other side, and she turns at the same time, and he draws her into the circle of his arms.

"I know what you want, I understand how you feel, but I can't do it, so please, Filly, don't ask me to."

She doesn't reply, but he can tell from the way she fits her body into his that she acquiesces to his request. She will never again ask him to accept treatment he hates and fears in order to stay alive for her a little longer.

And so they begin to live out their last months together. During the month of September, George is still fairly well. He uses this time to deal with the practicalities of death. He wants to teach Felicity all that she needs to know to live without him. He explains his system for saving information for tax purposes. He has an accountant to prepare the forms, but he needs the right information to work from. He advises her to work closely with their stock broker and to ask for help from their son Alfred whenever she needs advice about investments. He turns over all the paperwork of their health insurance policies to a professional woman who performs this service for a number of Meadows residents. George has an orderly mind, and the systems he has devised for taking care of their finances are well organized. He believes if he teaches them to Felicity, she will be able to manage without difficulty when he is no longer there. But she seems to resist his tutoring. Some times she hardly seems to be listening.

And he is right. She does not want to hear what he is saying, because just listening makes his approaching death feel real to her. If she can turn off what he is saying, she can also turn off that awful voice in her head that keeps repeating, "alone, alone, alone."

Sometime during that month Alfred comes from Boston to visit, and he promises George that whatever help Felicity needs later he will see that she gets it. George has known this all along, but it is a relief to him to hear it from Alfred now, and he stops his lessons with Felicity. The atmosphere in the apartment becomes less tense. In fact, although he is obviously losing weight and strength, George's mood becomes positively buoyant in early October. He tells his family that he has devised a schedule for the next weeks or as long as he is well enough to adhere to it.

"Felicity," he says, "I want you to take Saturdays off. Now, don't argue. You need some some R & R time—those pamphlets Dr. Craig's nurse gave us say so. And besides I want a little time alone with each of the children. So I suggest you spend the next few Saturdays with one of the children in New York or Boston while another one visits with me here at Meadows."

Felicity protests but she is outnumbered by George and the children, all of whom seem to have united solidly behind him. And so the following Friday night, their youngest daughter, Sally, comes to spend the night and to drive Felicity to the bus to Boston, where Alfred meets her. He takes her to his house in Weston, and after she has had a good visit with his wife, Cynthia, and their two young sons, he takes her into town for lunch at a prestigious restaurant and a tour of a Van Gogh exhibit at the Art Museum. At the bus station afterwards, she stands on tiptoe to kiss him goodbye.

"It's the best day I've had in weeks," she tells him, and realizes it's true.

She hopes George's day with Sally has gone as well, and as soon as she gets off the bus, she knows it has. Sally is glowing. "Oh, Mom," she says, "it was just the best day ever. We got to talk in ways we never have before. I never knew about his grandfather, his mom's dad, going bankrupt in the depression, and Gramps having to support him and his wife till they died."

Sally drops her at Meadows and leaves to drive back across the river to Troy. Upstairs Felicity finds George as elated as his daughter. They both start to talk at once, so eager are they to share their experiences with their children. "You were right, Toddy, one on one like today is just what we both need," says Felicity, and he replies, rather enigmatically, she thinks, "It does have its bonuses, even beyond what I thought." They agree to continue this program as long as he is able and the children are willing.

The following Saturday Sally comes again, and Felicity takes the train from Hudson to New York. It's a long trip, and so this weekend she will spend the night with Molly. George has given her instructions for Christmas presents for the children that she is to shop for while she is there. He wants gold charm bracelets for the girls, and he spells out what charms he wants for each: a horse for Molly who loved to ride when she was a child, a ballet dancer for Sally who took lessons for years—each charm he has listed has a meaning. He wants a gold pen and pencil set for Alfred that can be carried in his pocket or put on his desk in the elegant holder that comes with it.

"I thought you were going to give Alfred a gold watch. I mean, I thought you intended him to have yours."

"No, that's going to young George. He shares my initials, so he should have it. Besides, Alfred has a gold watch. Cynthia gave it to him as a wedding present when they were married."

"But little George is only four."

"I know that, Filly. But he won't always be four, and I want him to have it when he's older."

This was unusual behavior for George, a man who had always hated shopping for gifts or anything else for that matter, much less thinking about which ones might be appropriate for the recipients. He had given so many strange gifts over the years: a bathroom scale to her for their first anniversary, a vacuum cleaner for her birthday the first year they were married, a fishing pole in the year she was thirty when it should have been clear to anyone that she had no desire to fish—ever. These uninspired gifts and others have became family jokes, and as a result, he is uncomfortable trying to choose presents and has turned that responsibility over to her. And now he is taking care of his own

Christmas list without asking her advice. Obviously he is trying to do something special for what will be his last Christmas. She wonders what he has chosen for her and if he has commissioned one of the girls to purchase it.

The weekends continue as planned through October. It is the Todds' favorite season, and this year the tree color is especially beautiful in New England and the weather remains mild. By the end of the month all three children have had a long visit with both their parents. Molly tells George that they don't need Christmas presents, that these weekends have been the best presents they have ever received from him.

In November he begins to fade, slowly at first, but it is clear that he will not be with them much longer. Then his medication is changed, and for a while he recovers some of his strength. Felicity arranges a special Thanksgiving family dinner in the private dining room at Meadows. George is pushed there in a wheelchair and is able to sit at the head of the table. There are many toasts to him from his children, and the five grandchildren are on their best behavior. Molly, his stockbroker daughter, who also sings and plays the violin professionally for a church in New York, sings some of the old swing songs from the forties that George has always loved. And his sister brings some old home movies from the time of her own wedding in which Felicity and George are featured along with the bride and groom. By the end of the day he is exhausted but happy.

Felicity understands that what George wants and what he is trying his hardest to do, is to live through Christmas. He wants to be there to give his special gifts to his family. She talks to Dr Craig. "Will he make it?" she asks, but he doesn't know.

Afterwards Felicity thinks of December as the month of hospital equipment and nurses. Their bed is removed from the bedroom and a hospital bed replaces it. Felicity has a small folding cot brought from their storage area so she can continue to sleep in the room with him. She rents a commode in a chair to put beside his bed and an oxygen tank and respirator and a rack to hold I.V. bags. She also hires a nurse to come twice a day to give him shots, because now he is on a schedule of medications that he cannot take orally. The nurse also baths and shaves him. Felicity would like to do everything for him herself, but he is a big man and she doesn't know the professional techniques for turning him and making him comfortable.

At Christmas he is completely bedridden. There is much family discussion as to how they will have everyone together as he obviously desires. Finally they decide that Alfred and Sally will celebrate their family Christmas at their own homes with their children on Christmas Eve, and drive to Meadows for Christmas Day. Molly will come up a day earlier and spend the night with her parents and stay through the celebrations the next day. They arrange for a Christmas buffet at noon in the apartment so that they can carry their plates to the bedroom and eat with George.

Everything works out just as they have planned. The grandchildren visit with George when they first arrive, and he gives them their presents: cultured pearl necklaces for the girls, modern gold watches for the boys, except for young George who receives his grandfather's watch. Their parents explain that these are special gifts from their grandfather, not to wear now, but for later when they are older. Then the children go to the dining room where their parents have arranged plates of food for them. While they eat their food, their parents go to his bedroom to eat with George and open their presents from him.

Molly and Sally love their bracelets. They see that George has chosen charms that have special significance for each of them. Alfred is delighted with the pen and pencil set, and the lapis necklace is a perfect match for Cynthia's dark blue eyes. Sally's husband, Frank, a tech researcher, opens a package containing some gadget that is a total mystery to Felicity, but he is obviously impressed. "How did you know? Where did you find it?" he keeps asking George.

Then it is Felicity's turn. She knows her present is jewelry because the package is so small. She opens it slowly while George watches her with a brighter expression on his face than she has seen in weeks. She knows that he is waiting for her reaction, and she promises herself that she will show enthusiasm no matter what she might feel. But when she opens the box, what she sees is a gold pin in the shape of a daffodil. It is a pretty piece of jewelry, but she is puzzled as to why he chose it. She doesn't particularly like pins and rarely wears the ones she has. But she smiles broadly and says as brightly as she can, "How beautiful, darling, I'll think of you whenever I wear it," and rises to go to him and kiss him. Although he knows her so well, he doesn't seem to pick up on her failure to understand its significance, whatever it may be. In fact, he seems enormously pleased by his gift to her.

After Christmas George seems to give up. Although he doesn't say so, he makes it clear that he is ready to die. He lies in his bed with his eyes closed and seldom speaks except to ask for ice for his dry mouth. Then he stops speaking altogether and goes into a coma, and on the first day of the new year, he inhales one long last rasping breath and is gone.

Felicity remembers very little of the funeral or the days just before it. Later when she reads the program given out at the church, she wonders if she was even there. She misses George as if he had been her sight or one of her limbs. She feels incomplete, and she knows that she will never again be the whole person that she was with him. She cries in her bed at night, and takes long afternoon naps. She comes down with a terrible cold that turns into pneumonia, and sometimes she thinks of the pain pills that are left from George's illness and wonders whether, if she took them all, they might give her the oblivion she craves. Her children are concerned, and her pneumonia is the last straw. When she recovers, they insist she go south to her sister's house in Sarasota for the rest of the winter.

The warm weather and the company of her sister, who is also her dearest friend, begin the process of healing. The two women take long walks on the beach, and Sarah, who has been a widow for several years, has comfort to offer. She understands Felicity's pain even better than her children do. She promises Felicity that it will diminish with time, something Felicity does not really believe, but it makes her feel better to hear Sarah say so.

In mid April, she returns north. Sally meets her at the Albany airport and drives her to Meadows. They go up in the elevator to the apartment, and Sally opens the doors to the balcony, to air out the place, she says, as she walks out to survey the landscape. When she comes back in, she is full of suppressed excitement. She wants Felicity to come on a walk with her. There is something her mother must see, and though she has just arrived, it can't wait. It must be seen now. She bundles Felicity back into the coat she has just taken off, and leads her down and out of the building and onto a walkway that leads to the path on the circumference of the property.

They walk about a hundred yards, and Felicity can see something new on the path where she and George used to walk together. As she gets closer she realizes that there is a huge planting of daffodils ahead on either side of the path, probably a thousand or more. The sun has brought most of them into bloom, and they are beautiful to behold, yellow with long white cups that have a tiny line of red at their edges. She has never seen any like them before. A new variety, she thinks. There is a widening of the path in their midst, and a new Luydens garden bench has been placed on it. She sinks onto it to look at the blossoms all around her, but Sally pulls her to her feet again.

"Where did they come from?" she asks her daughter.

"Oh, Mom," says Sally, who is laughing with excitement, "look at the plaque on the bench."

And so she turns and reads the little brass plaque that is screwed to the bench.

*For my Felicity, to celebrate our life together,*
*A field of Felicities to tell you I love you, Toddy*

She still doesn't completely understand. "What does it mean, a field of Felicities? It doesn't make sense."

"Mom, they're Felicity daffodils. That's their name. When Daddy saw a reference to them in a travel article about Holland, he had to have them for you. At first he wanted just a few for your little garden plot, but then he thought of doing this. He got approval from the Meadows Board, and we put them in last fall. You can see them from your balcony, you know. He arranged for them to be planted where you could."

"But how did he do it without my knowing?" But even as she spoke, she knew.

"We all worked on it. Even Daddy was able to do some of it, dropping bulbs in the holes we dug. Alfred was wonderful, twice as fast as I, and Molly did her part by taking care of you, which she much preferred to digging holes, but she did that too when it was her turn to have time alone with Daddy."

Sally picks her a big bunch of the flowers to take back to the apartment. "Nobody else is supposed to pick them, just you. Daddy got that agreement from the Board before they were put in. I guess since I'm picking them for you, it's okay."

They walk back to the apartment, and after a cup of tea, Sally leaves and Felicity is alone again. She puts on her coat and goes out to sit on the balcony. Sally is right. She can see the daffodils from here. There is a breeze, and the flower heads are bobbing as it blows through them. She feels as if they are speaking to her for George, saying, I love you.

Then she remembers the pin he gave her for Christmas. She has never worn it. All the time she was in Florida, it stayed here in her bureau. Now she understands why he gave it to her. She presses her face into the bouquet that Sally picked for her and breathes in its sweet fragrance. And for the first time in months, she is able to think of herself as one of the lucky ones again.

# Sophie and Andrew

The Rothmans live on the second floor in a C model apartment. They chose it, or rather Andrew chose it, because it faces west, and from the balcony, they can see the bell tower of the chapel on the campus. Not being a gardener, he failed to realize that orientation is often more important than view. Consequently, when he has his two fingers of Scotch before dinner, he cannot sit on the balcony to drink it because the western sun is merciless. This is a great frustration to him. A small matter you might think, but it is just one more bit of pain added to his already overflowing cup.

His wife, Sophie, has Alzheimer's. Every day he watches her slow decline, and it is breaking his heart. He forces himself to be stoical, and to all appearances he is. Everyone at Meadows admires his courage and the care he takes of her. They don't know that at night when he has finally got her to bed and has checked to see that she is asleep and all the doors are locked, he goes into the bathroom and weeps quietly in the shower.

The C models have two bedrooms and two baths. Andrew sleeps in the room with Sophie, although no longer in the same bed. She is so restless at night that he uses a cot which he pulls across the threshold of the room to prevent her from wandering. If she goes out into living room, she doesn't know where she is and she begins to wail piteously. He always rescues her quickly, but he can't bear to hear the terror in her sobs. He has discovered that it is easier to block her way with the cot. The second bedroom has become his study.

He has worked out a schedule that is at least keeping him sane. His children have insisted that he must take care of himself as well as Sophie. Sometimes in his darker moments he wonders if their real concern is that if he can no longer care for her, they will have to take over the burden. He tries to push such thoughts aside, but he knows very well that if he collapses, they will put her in a nursing home. They are not selfish children. In fact, they are better than most, but they have many responsibilities of their own—children, careers, households to run. They cannot take on Sophie as well.

For Sophie requires a great deal of care. Andrew has arranged for a woman to come in at noon every day to make her lunch and sit with her while she eats and stay with her through the afternoon. Her name is Lucy, a Jamaican, whose voice makes Andrew think of a musical instrument. He can't remember the name, some hollow wooden tube that you run a stick up and down to make a melody. He can hear the sound of it in his head when Lucy talks to Sophie.

As soon as she arrives, Andrew goes down to the dining room where he has his main meal of the day. This is his chance to socialize with other residents who often invite him to sit with them. He is an attractive, well-spoken man, and they enjoy his company. Afterwards he usually joins a threesome of new friends that he has met since he moved to Meadows for a bridge game in the card room.

When they first moved to High Meadows he used to take Sophie to the dining room for dinner, and they were often invited to join other residents at their tables. Sophie didn't speak often, but she sat in her chair and smiled, and sometimes when every one laughed, she laughed too, although Andrew knew she didn't understand the joke. But she has deteriorated in the last six months and no one asks them to dine any more. It's not that the residents are cruel. They simply don't know how to deal with Sophie as she is now. Sometimes she babbles to herself. Sometimes she gets up to wander and Andrew has to go after her. He understands why no one wants to sit with her, but it hurts him that no one here will ever know her as she once was, in all her magnificence.

The only public gathering that he still takes Sophie to is the Thursday afternoon tea in the large living room on the main floor. She loves the music, which is provided by the Dunham sisters, three residents of Meadows who are fine musicians. Abby Dunham plays the grand piano, and her sisters play the cello and the violin. Andrew finds an inconspicuous corner, and he and Sophie sit and listen. Lucy always sees that Sophie's hair is done Thursdays, and she dresses her in one of her prettiest dresses at teatime. She even applies light make-up to Sophie's face. She is proud of her charge and wants her always to be seen at her best advantage.

Sophie is Russian. Andrew has always enjoyed telling the tale of their meeting which took place in Paris where Andrew had gone to size up a ballet company from Moscow for a possible engagement at the Philadelphia Performing Arts Center where he was the booking agent.

"Sophie was a member of the ensemble, but I could see that she was already something special. She seemed to dance in the air above the stage. And she was beautiful, so beautiful. I was supposed to be assessing the whole company, but I couldn't see anybody but Sophie. After the performance I bribed the stage manager to take me backstage and introduce me to her. She couldn't speak English, but we learned to communicate with smiles and later with kisses. This was during the height of the Cold War, and fraternization between Russian citizens and Americans was strictly forbidden by the Russian Government, so you can imagine how dangerous it was for her to even speak to me, but I managed to see her several times. Then on the night of the ballet's final performance, I smuggled her into the American Embassy, where I used all the influence I could muster to get her refugee status and a visa to the United States. We were married as soon as we got to Philadelphia. I wasn't surprised when I arrived home to find a cable from the ballet company refusing the contract I had offered them."

It is a romantic story, and his listeners usually enjoyed hearing him tell it, but recently he has realized that the contrast between the beautiful ballerina of the story and what Sophie has become makes his audience too uncomfortable.

Sophie danced in the U.S. with several ballet companies, but when she was only forty, she began to develop severe arthritis in her hands. Gnarled and swollen finger joints precluded any further performances, but she established a ballet school which became well known and was eventually absorbed into the fine arts program at the University of Pennsylvania. However, she remained frustrated by her inability to dance herself. She missed the excitement of performing before an audience, and it saddened Andrew to see her obvious unhappiness.

Andrew himself had been an enthusiastic amateur ballroom dancer, and he and Sophie danced together well. It occurred to him that they could polish their skills and enter some of the ballroom dancing contests that were becoming popular around the country. He believed she might recover some of the joie de vivre she felt when she danced, even though it was not her beloved ballet.

And so he hired a coach and the three of them worked to perfect a number of routines representing several styles of dancing. Through his theatrical contacts he was able to arrange for the requisite spectacular ball gowns for Sophie, and somehow they found time to practice in spite of their busy schedules. The first time they competed they were thrilled to win a second, and from that time on, they almost always placed among the winners. Ballroom dancing became an obsession for both of them, and as their children grew up and moved out, they devoted more and more of their lives to it.

But when Sophie reached her early sixties, she began to have trouble learning new dance routines. She had no problem with the old ones, but it was important in the dance competitions to have something new for each contest. At first Andrew thought that she just wasn't concentrating, and he became annoyed with her. Later when he realized that her problems were the first sign of her Alzheimer's, he reproached himself for his earlier impatience.

Slowly in the beginning, then at accelerated speed, he has watched the person he loves fade away. She seems to have gone inward into the past. Some days she speaks to him in Russian, which he does not understand. Occasionally she sings to herself a tuneless la-la-la. Sometimes he watches her fill in all the spaces in a crossword puzzle with x's which she then proudly shows him.

But more disturbing to him than the disintegration of her mind and of what he thinks of as her essence are those moments when she seems briefly to be herself again. They still occur, but ever more rarely. Only last week she turned to him suddenly and said, "Andy, dear, I do love it when you wear that blue shirt. It matches your eyes." Her face was alert, her eyes bright, and in the moment before her expression faded to the usual one, which to him seems like that of a lost child, for just that moment he thought as he always does, that she was healed, that he had her back again. The letdown from those seconds of hope are so painful that tears spring to his eyes.

Sometimes in the evening they watch television. She particularly seems to like ice dancing, and so he has bought a video of the Olympic finals of both singles and pairs skaters. She watches attentively. On one occasion she stood up and assumed the position of a skater on the screen who was gliding across the ice on one skate, her other leg extended straight behind her, both arms out stretched to the side, her head held up. It is a pose that Sophie often took in the ballet, and it showed off her beautiful, long, slender neck. Before he could comment (he wanted to tell her she looked like a swan), the music changed to a fast-paced rendition of *Bolero*. It was a piece they used for one of their favorite routines, and he could see she recognized it, for she began to move her feet in the dance they created for it. On impulse he rose and extended his arms in an invitation. Without hesitation she stepped into them, and they began to dance together. It had been a long time since they did this particular dance, but her body had forgotten nothing, nor, he soon discovered, had his. Although the living room was a small space, and pieces of furniture presented obstacles where there should have been none, he found that he could improvise moves to avoid them, and she followed. It was vibrant, passionate music, and their dance mirrored its sound.

When the music at last ended, they were both breathless, but she nevertheless turned to an imaginary audience and curtsied deeply. Then she turned to him as she used to do and curtsied again. He was in rapture to see her thus replay their glory days, but when she rose to face him, it was with the dull eyes and sagging body that he had come to know all too well.

Still, he wonders now if dancing might not be a form of therapy for her, and he arranges to rent a studio at the college for the remaining months of summer. He goes to the storage area to retrieve their dancing shoes from a trunk that also contains some of the gowns she wore when they danced. He lifts them out to examine them and catches his breath at the scent of her perfume, released into the air of the small compartment. Here are mementos of their happy years together: the yellow silk taffeta for their Viennese waltz number for which they won a first, the pink chiffon decorated with yards and yards of maribou, the red and black costume trimmed in gold coins that was made for the Spanish dance they created for the *Bolero* performance. She will never wear them again, he thinks sadly; I may as well dispose of them. But for now he takes only her sandals and his pumps and leaves the rest.

He plans to take her the next morning to the studio, but while he is shaving, she escapes from his supervision and walks out into the hallway wearing only her nightgown, with her hair uncombed and her feet bare. He is frantic. There are so many corridors to wander, so many stairways to ascend or descend. He has no idea where to begin looking for her, and so he is obliged to call the staff and enlist their help, although it pains him to expose her to their attention. There have already been suggestions that she might be better off if he put her in the Alzheimer's wing of the nursing home. He knows in his heart it may eventually come to that, but not yet, not yet, he tells himself.

They find her in a stairwell in another wing of the building, cowering on a landing and crying. There is another hint from the manager as Andrew leads her away. He is in despair. He hates for anyone to see her like this when he knows how glorious she was, how glorious she can be even now. Back at the apartment he unlocks the door to their balcony and leads her out on to it. He hopes the balmy spring air will help her recover her composure.

"Look, Sophie," he says. "Look over there at the beautiful daffodil garden. See, they're moving in the breeze, like a troupe of ballerinas."

She begins to become quieter. She has always loved flowers and the sight of this display begins to calm her. "Yellow," she says, "yellow waltzers."

If he had not seen the yellow silk dress so recently, he would not have made the connection.

"Yes, my darling," he says, "yellow waltzers."

He leads her back inside and helps her dress and then takes her to the studio to dance. When the music begins, she forgets her panic back at the Meadows building. Her back straightens, and her long neck stretches, her arms and legs assume the correct position, and together they dance the Bolero number. They never miss a step, and Sophie actually looks happy, and so the studio dancing becomes a daily routine for them.

At a Thursday tea not long afterwards, there is an unusually large attendance of the residents. For the first time this year it is warm enough to open the French doors onto the broad deck that links the reception room to the gardens beyond. Chairs and tables have been set around the edge, and the overflow from inside is sitting there. Andrew has found seats for himself and Sophie in a corner of the deck, and they are listening to a Mozart concerto with much pleasure. When it is done, the Dunhams begin a very different piece; it is Bizet's *Bolero*.

Sophie is suddenly alert. She looks at Andrew with an inquiring expression on her face, then rises and holds out her hand to him, and he rises to stand before her. He takes her left hand in his right and places his own left hand on her back. He can feel the instant response of her body and see the excitement leap in her eyes, and he turns her in a circle so that all the residents on the deck can see her. And then they are off twirling across the deck in perfect synchronization.

Their audience is dumbfounded. Those who are still inside in the reception room flood out onto the deck where they crowd against the wall to make room for the dancers.

They have heard that Sophie was once a fine ballerina, but they had no idea that either she or Andrew had this remarkable talent for ballroom dancing.

Andrew is doing what he always did when they danced; he is showcasing Sophie. After all she is the truly talented one, the ballerina who studied from childhood to dance in one of Russia's great companies. He was no more than a better than average social dancer when they began. It is she who patiently taught him and encouraged him and was ultimately responsible for their success. Their coach knew that Sophie was the star of the partnership and choreographed their dances accordingly. Although judges admired Andrew's competence, they awarded prizes to the couple because Sophie dancing was a sight glorious to behold.

One last time he is making her the star. He leads her with his hands and his body. He pushes her away and draws her back and sends her twirling around him. He holds her hand high above her head, and she spins around beneath it. He bends her backwards and feels her arch her back and thrust her chin high until her long shapely neck is fully extended. Always he keeps contact, her hand in his or his on her body. He thinks if he lets go of her, even for an instant, she will crumple away.

Their audience now knows what a special spectacle this is. They are hushed now, afraid to break what is truly a spell. But Sophie is aware of their presence, and whatever she consciously makes of it, she feels it as a state of grace. She soaks up their awe and admiration and turns it into energy and passion. Andrew knows that they were better dancers in their prime, but never have they given their audience such a magnificent performance.

Then it is over. The music is done. Sophie gives the audience her deep graceful curtsey and turns to Andrew to repeat it. And at that moment he signals to Lucy who has been watching and now steps forward with a wrap which she drapes over Sophie's shoulders just as she begins to sag into her familiar slumped posture. Andrew kisses her, and Lucy leads her away to an elevator that takes them up to the apartment.

Now the residents are applauding and cheering. They are standing, some with the aid of canes or walkers, and crying "Bravo!" Andrew walks into the midst of them. He bows and raises his arms for silence.

"I know," he says, when they are finally quiet, "I know your cheers are for Sophie, but she has returned to that strange land in which she lives when she is not dancing. None of us, not even I who love her so dearly, can go there with her, nor would we wish to. Today she has given you a glimpse of who she used to be, a truly great performer, *une artiste extraordinaire*, and at this, her last performance, you have given her the gifts that a great artist requires above all others. You have given her your attention, your recognition, and above all else your love and understanding, and I thank you for her with all my heart."

He leaves the room, although they are beginning to applaud again, and starts back to join Sophie in the apartment. In the elevator he leans against the wall. Now that it's over, he can feel how much this unexpected performance has drained him. Tomorrow once again, the residents will see Sophie shuffling along on her walk with Lucy, barely aware herself of who she is, but, he thinks, now at least they know, *they know.*

# The Dunham Sisters

In one of the cottages on the grounds of High Meadows live the three Dunham sisters. They have come here from Manchester, Vermont where they were much loved, much respected teachers in the local school system for almost fifty years. Mothers waited anxiously all summer, hoping that their children would be assigned to one of the Misses Dunham. Those whose children were placed with other teachers called the principal to protest or to beg for their reassignment. It was an ordeal the principal dreaded every year.

The sisters grew up in Manchester, where their father owned a small shoe manufacturing business. After college they returned to their hometown to teach in the lower grades of the public schools. They loved the children, and the children adored them. There were a number of suitors in their earlier years, for they were all comely young women with cheerful personalities, but apparently no man could arouse in any of them the passion they felt for their young charges, and so they remained single, living with their father in the house where they were born. Most people forgot that Abby had been engaged to a young soldier who died in the invasion of Iwo Jima, and only her sisters knew that Beth had had a long love affair with a married man who lived in the Adirondacks where she managed a girls' camp for many summers. Jennie, the youngest and prettiest, had several opportunities to marry, but no one quite suited, and Jennie too remained a spinster. They sublimated their maternal instincts with their love for their students, especially Jennie, who referred to her kindergarteners as her "babies." Soon after Jennie retired, they decided to move together to High Meadows.

The sisters' good looks are apparent even now, and their dispositions are as pleasant as ever. There is a strong family resemblance among them, as they all have the same fine skin, rosy apple cheeks, retrousee noses, and small even teeth. Yet they are never mistaken for one another, for there are clear differences among them. Abby, the eldest, is tall, and her hair is short and quite white. Beth is jolly and always smiling and has blue eyes like Abby's. Jennie has large brown eyes and is the most outgoing.

But although there are these differences in their appearances, as in many families, their voices and their laughs are almost identical. If you were to walk down a hallway in the main building and hear one of them speaking in an intersecting corridor, you would have no idea which sister was approaching until you turned the corner. Nor can you guess who is answering the phone when you call. And they are all musical. They have lovely singing voices and are often asked to perform some of their harmonic repertory or to play their instruments for the residents on special occasions.

Beth is two years younger than Abby, who is seventy-nine, and Jennie, often referred to by the older sisters as "mama's afterthought," is only sixty-seven. She was their adored pet when she was little, and it is obvious to everyone that they still treasure her. In some ways they are almost like parents, always looking out for her welfare.

They are happy at High Meadows, but they miss the children they used to teach, and they look forward to weekends when children come to visit their grandparents.

"I never wanted children of my own when we were teaching." says Jennie to her sisters one Sunday in the dining room. "After all, I had my babies then. But sometimes now I wish I had grandchildren. Just look at that little girl of the Nelsons. She must be a first grader. See how she is trying to read the menu. And she keeps patting Elsie's arm to show her she can read. Oh, I wish Elsie would pay attention. There's nothing like a little praise to encourage a child who's trying to learn."

Abby is smiling as she watches a little boy at the next table. "Do you see that young grandson of the Nelsons? He's a real little devil. He's been putting his vegetables in the napkin in his lap so he won't have to eat them, and Irma Nelson hasn't a clue what he's up to. I always loved little boys with spirit. They were a challenge, but I felt they added spice to my classroom." She thinks, as she always does when she sees a red-headed, freckled young boy, of her long dead soldier and the child they might have had.

"Having grandchildren must be wonderful even when they get to that awkward adolescent stage", says Beth, as they watch the gawky grandson of a very old lady lead her to her chair and carefully seat her.

One day in April, when Jennie is taking her daily walk on the circumference path of the Meadows property (so much more pleasant now that spring is coming), she sees ahead the daffodil garden that a resident created to honor his wife. In the last few days, it has burst into bloom, a sea of fluttering yellow and white set in motion by the wind. There is a bench just off the path, and she plans to sit down for a little while to admire the beauty of the flowers, but then she sees that someone else is already there. She starts to walk past, but he has seen her hesitate and moves over, gesturing for her to sit down.

She recognizes him as someone she has met, but with whom she has never really conversed. He is John Loreo, a relative newcomer to Meadows. He moved here three months ago shortly after his wife died, a sad man unable to deal with his loss. He can speak of nothing but Heloise and her fine qualities and of how he misses her. He praises her courage during the months of her long, slow death from Parkinson's disease. Just the mention of her name brings tears to his eyes. When he first arrived, he was the object of a good deal of sympathy from members of the community, but now that he has been here a few months and shows no sign of "moving on with his life," their patience has eroded, and they mostly avoid him. Pain and suffering and death are not popular subjects with the Meadows population; they do not wish to dwell on what the future holds for them. Denial and a stiff upper lip and, at the least, silence are considered the proper responses to loss and other tragedies.

Jennie is feeling particularly light-hearted this spring morning, and, knowing John Loreo's reputation, much as she wants to sit and admire the daffodils, she does not want to sit with him and listen to the sad recital of his wife's good qualities. But it seems churlish to refuse his invitation, and so she takes the place on the bench that he indicates.

"You're one of the Dunham sisters, aren't you?" he says. "I'm John Loreo. We've only met briefly, but of course I've seen you about, and I heard you and your sisters sing at the Palm Sunday program last week. You were wonderful."

"I like that hymn too. We used to sing it at our church in Manchester."

"My wife Heloise had a fine voice. I used to love to hear her sing."

Oh, dear, thinks Jennie, here he goes.

But he surprises her by turning on the bench to point out to her the plaque on its back.

"Have you seen this?" he asks. "It's interesting to me because the daffodil garden was planted by a dying man for his wife. Usually it's the living who memorialize the dead. But he planted these daffodils when he was ill to remind her later of how much he loved her. Don't you think that's beautiful?"

Jennie, who knows the story of the garden, agrees that it is indeed a beautiful idea.

"I don't know much about flowers and gardens," he says. "What will be here after the daffodils have finished blooming?"

"Well, I don't know," says Jennie. "I guess the area will be mulched and kept weeded. I don't think there are any other flowers in this bed."

"I've been sitting here wondering if I could add something for Heloise. Maybe a bench over there in the shade for people to use in the summer. Are there flowers that could be planted in the shade? Maybe some kind of summer flowers could replace the daffodils when they die. Would it hurt them to plant other flowers where they are now? You wouldn't have to dig them up or anything, would you?"

"What a wonderful idea! A bench under that tree would be perfect. Walkers who get hot and tired in summer could take a break in the shade. It would be just the place for a shade garden. Ferns, if you want it all green, or there are lots of flowering plants that like the shade if you want more color." Jennie is already beginning to envision a shade garden here and annuals where the daffodils are blooming now. She can imagine those new petunias that bloom all summer and blue ageratum and something white, nicotiana perhaps.

John sees her excitement and smiles at her. She realizes she has seen him many times but never smiling. And that is a pity, for he has a beguiling smile that transforms his whole face. He smiles with his mouth and his eyes and with his eyebrows, which shoot up into high arches above his eyes. She is so surprised by this sudden transformation that she laughs out loud, and he begins to laugh as well.

"If I arrange to do this garden," he asks, "will you help plan it?"

"Yes," she says, "yes, of course I will."

And that is the beginning of a friendship that soon becomes a romance.

This affair is watched with much delight by the residents of Meadows. They see, sooner than they could have imagined possible, the transformation of John Loreo from a mournful widower to a starstruck lover. He is like an adolescent boy experiencing his first love. "What a change," they say to one another, smiling slyly. This love affair lifts their spirits. It makes the present sweet and offers them the possibility of a sweeter future. Perhaps the poet was right, they think, "The best is yet to be." For a little while their fears for what lies ahead are vanquished by the recurring sight of an elderly man holding hands with a slightly younger spinster lady. Not yet, they think, not yet.

Not quite everyone is totally happy about their affair. Abby and Beth have ambivalent feelings. For so long it has been the three of them, and it is hard for them to think of it being otherwise. They have always looked after Jennie, the baby sister, and now someone else wants to take over her care. They scarcely realize that recently Jennie has been gradually becoming their caretaker in many small ways. It is she who finds their missing glasses, reminds them to take their medicines, puts their clothing in mothballs for summer, and performs many other small services for them. At the same time they are vaguely aware that if anything happens to one of the older sisters, they are counting on Jennie being there for the survivor. Neither of them has ever worried about being left alone. Now that security is threatened by Jennie's devotion to John Loreo.

Yet how can they be so selfish, they ask each other, when Jennie is so radiantly happy. They have always loved her so, always wanted the best for her, the best being whatever she wanted for herself. Now she is joyful in a way they have never seen before. They resolve to put aside their own confused feelings and give her their blessings. After all, they tell each other, it's not as if she's going away. She and John will be living right here at Meadows.

The courtship is short. John wants Jennie to marry him as soon as possible. "Who knows at our age?" he says, more than once, and Jennie understands. He is seventy-seven after all, and he wants to spend all the time he has with her.

On weekends he takes her to meet his five children and their families, all except Robert in California and Mary in London. "They'll be here for the wedding," he tells her, "but such a large family can be overwhelming, especially with all the twelve grandchildren. I thought you might rather meet the families one at a time."

Jennie agrees, although quite naturally she is nervous about meeting his children, even one by one. Perhaps they won't like their father marrying again less than six months after their mother's death, she thinks. Perhaps they won't like her. Perhaps she will never fit into a family so large with all its own history, its own stories and jokes. But she goes with him, and all the visits go surprisingly well. Clearly there is no resentment. Rather they are obviously delighted that she is making their father so happy. She finds it strange, however, that both his son Paul and his daughter Angela go out of their way to mention to her privately that their mother had been a difficult person. Listening to John speak of her, Jennie had conjured up her own image of Heloise as a perfect wife and mother. Now she is confused, but she can scarcely ask John for clarification.

They decide that the wedding will be limited to family. It is impossible to single out a small number of the Meadows residents for inclusion without offending the rest. And there are other friends from Manchester and from Worchester, John's home before he came to Meadows.

"Only your sisters? And all my big family? There's my sister Eleanor, too, you know, Jennie, and her children and grandchildren. They'll all expect to come. Don't you have some cousins you would like to invite? It doesn't seem right to have just your two sisters for you."

But Jennie assures him that she has no cousins and that the presence of Abby and Beth is all that she desires.

The weekend of the wedding, the Lareo family descends on the town en mass. They are a noisy bunch, all together in the small local inn where they talk and laugh and exchange family news, all the while chasing small children or fishing them out of the swimming pool. To the Dunhams, who have come with John to join them for a picnic lunch, the scene is chaotic, but once the children are seated and served with food, it becomes more orderly. The sisters are introduced to everyone, and John's children make a point of telling Abby and Beth how happy they are for their father that he has found Jennie.

"She's the perfect person for him," they tell her sisters. "He's been so lonely since Mother died. He needs someone to look after and love."

After lunch John sits beside Jennie and smiles his wonderful smile at the scene before him. "Look," he says to Jennie who is holding the youngest Loreo in her lap and trying to divert her baby fingers from the pearl necklace that is her wedding present from John. At one picnic table Abby is sitting with the older grandchildren, telling them one of her famous ghost stories. They are totally enthralled. On the lawn Beth is conducting the smaller grandchildren in a game of Loosey-Goosey. Her laughter rings out as loud as the children's.

"I think my grandchildren are being blessed with three new grandmothers," John says.

Jennie knows that he is welcoming her sisters into his family. She thinks of how happy they will be when she repeats to them what he has just said, and she presses his hand and kisses him on the cheek.

That evening John hosts a formal dinner party, as formal, that is, as it is possible to make a party that includes seventeen young children, for his sister, Eleanor, has arrived with her family, including her five grandchildren. There are many toasts and welcoming speeches and laughter. There is even a toast by thirteen year old Mitch, who is John's oldest grandchild. He stands up and says that he speaks for all of his generation in welcoming "the three Dunham ladies" into the family and that he hopes they will all consent to be honorary grandmothers. There is loud applause by adults and children alike, and Jennie can see that her sisters are touched. She knows that John has put the boy up to this toast, but she can also see that Mitch's sentiments are genuine.

Later she slips out onto the broad terrace that adjoins the private dinning room where the dinner is served. This is her last night alone, and she wants to reflect quietly on the changes that have occurred in her life in the last few months. She has few qualms about this marriage. She believes that it is right for them both, and she recognizes how strong her feelings for John have become in such a short time. She does sometimes wonder how she can ever fill the shoes of the formidably perfect Heloise. And she sometimes wonders how John, who was so distraught by Heloise's death, can have transferred his affections to someone else, to *her*, so soon. It is a mystery that she struggles often to resolve, and she promises herself that this is the last time, that after tomorrow she will accept his love for her without question.

She walks to the edge of the terrace. It is dusk and an orange moon is visible through the branches of the old oak trees that rim the blue stone patio. Behind the mountains to the west, the last pink and gold light from the sunset is still streaking the darkening sky where a few early stars can be seen. Voices and laughter and the sound of a piano float out from the dinning room, too soft to interfere with her thoughts.

But before she can begin to consider the problem, Eleanor walks out of the party and joins her.

"No second thoughts, I hope?" she says to Jennie.

"Oh, no, none at all. Everyone in John's family has been so welcoming to me. In fact, I've wondered...Her voice trails off.

"I suspect you wonder why everyone is so happy that John is marrying you so soon after Heloise's death when he has been so distraught at loosing her."

"Well, something like that, I guess."

"Don't worry, Jennie. I'm sure you probably believe, listening to John, that St. Heloise was perfect, and wonder how you can fill her shoes."

Jennie is shocked at the tone of Eleanor' voice. Is she being sarcastic? Jennie hardly knows how to respond. She has just met this sister of John's this evening, and she isn't sure how to interpret what she says.

"But he loved her so much," she finally manages to say.

"Of course he did," says Eleanor. "That's John's great talent, unconditional love. He's just like our father. Daddy loved Mother and John and me and all his other family and friends as if we were perfect, and you can be sure we weren't. Poor Mother was an alcoholic, and I was lazy and sloppy—never to be depended on—in short, a mess."

"And John? Surely John wasn't a problem?"

"No, you're right. John was never a problem. Like Daddy, he loved us all so much that he spent his childhood trying to please us. It's frightening, you know, that kind of all embracing, all forgiving love. After Daddy died, John took up his role as caretaker protector. It's hard to live up to love like that when you know you're flawed. So I think Mother and I were actually glad when he married Heloise. I think we both thought, let her cope with it. Poor Heloise. I've never known anyone so lacking in self-esteem. He spent his life with her trying to love her so much that she would love herself. He praised everything she did, but he only succeeded in convincing himself that she was perfect. His love for her was like a flood of water pouring into a desert. The sand absorbs it all and still remains arid.

"The funny thing is that after he left home to marry, Mother overcame her alcoholism almost right away, and I discovered the meaning of responsibility. There wasn't anyone anymore to cosset us, to pick up the pieces when we fell apart, as Daddy and then John had done, so we somehow found the courage to change ourselves. Yes, John's marriage was the making of me."

Jennie is appalled. "Are you saying that marriage to John will be a mistake?" she asks.

"No, of course not. You misunderstand me. A person like John lives to love. I'm so happy that John has finally found someone who's worthy of that love. After your visits to his children, they all wrote me that you were a beautiful strong person. I simply want you to know that Heloise's reputation is nothing that you have to live up to. John may spend the rest of his life thinking she was something she never was, but I can assure you that you are already on an even higher pedestal. It is clear to all his family that you love him very much, and it gives us all joy to see his great love finally reciprocated." She crosses to where Jennie is standing and kisses her cheek and walks back into the dining room.

In just these few minutes the sky has darkened, and the colors that were visible when Jennie came out on the terrace have faded away. The moon, now a disc of pearl, has risen above the trees, wisps of pale clouds float across a gray sky, and a host of stars have joined the early ones. Jennie sits on a chair and considers what Eleanor has just told her. She understands that Eleanor is both warning her and encouraging her. She is telling her that John's great capacity for loving makes him vulnerable to those he loves and allows them to be less than they can be, but that it can be a blessing to those who return it unselfishly.

She understands now how John has fallen in love with her so soon after losing Heloise. He needs a living object for his love and she is it. She promises herself that she will never abuse that love. She feels at that moment a great wave of affection for him, for his goodness and unselfishness. All her uncertainties are gone.

She looks up from where she is sitting and sees him in a doorway into the dining room, silhouetted against the light. He is looking out on the terrace, looking for her, she knows, unable to see her in the darkness. She jumps up and calls to him. "John, John, here I am. I'm coming," and runs toward him and all the joyous sounds of the party inside.

# Katherine and Charlie

When Katherine Bagley comes home to her apartment at High Meadows from grocery shopping and finds her husband Charles slumped in his chair in the living room with his head falling to one side and a bewildered expression on his face, she has no idea at first that he has had a stroke.

"Charlie," she cries, "what's wrong? Is it one of the girls?" It never occurs to her that anything could be wrong with *him*.

He tries to answer her. His lips twitch in an effort to speak, but he can manage no more than a long drawn out "uhhhhhhhh." His left arm, which has been resting on the arm of his chair, falls to the side and dangles uselessly.

Katherine drops her groceries and rushes to his side. She tries to pull his body into a more upright position, but she finds she is not strong enough to move him, for although he is not a large man, she is a very small woman.

Charlie is looking at her questioningly and she can see how afraid he is. For a moment she, too, is paralyzed by fear, but for his sake she suppresses her terror and composes her face. In a voice as calm as she can muster, she says, "Don't worry, darling. I'll call Henry. He'll know what to do." She rushes to the phone and calls first 911 and then their family doctor and good friend, Henry Bell.

Then she sits on the chair edge and pulls his head into the circle of her arms. She smoothes his hair and murmurs encouragements until an ambulance arrives and takes them both to the hospital. And there—thank God—is Henry. He is in his golf clothes, and for a moment she feels remorse at having taken him away from his Saturday morning game. But then she thinks, what else are doctors or good friends for, if not to be there for you when you need them?

The emergency room doctor examines Charlie quickly. Katherine goes to the office to fill out the necessary papers, and when she returns, Charlie has been moved and Henry is waiting for her. He sees the look of panic on her face at the sight of the empty room and hastens to reassure her.

"I sent him for a cat scan, and from there he'll go into coronary care," he tells her. "He's had a stroke. It's hard to know what kind it is—we have to do some tests. We'll know a lot more when we have his scans and his blood tests back and after we've had a chance to observe his progress or lack of it. There's medication that usually helps if the stroke victim gets it soon enough, but we need to know what kind of a stroke this is before we can give it to him."

He has been speaking as Dr. Bell, but now he puts his arm around her, and he is just Henry, Charlie's oldest friend and confidant, his roommate at college, his former tennis partner, and the person Charlie loves best in the world after his own family. The Bells and the Bagleys have vacationed together at the Bagley's Cape Cod cottage, gone together to Elderhostels, and worried about their children together. Kate and Charlie are at High Meadows in this town where Henry still practices because Henry and his wife Jean moved in here first and urged the Bagleys to join them. Short and stout with a fringe of white hair around his bald head, he is one of the last of the old-fashioned doctors who try to make adequate time for all their patients. Now he is looking at Katherine, his usually genial face full of concern, and she realizes that it is for her. For a moment she feels panic for what may lie ahead, but she refuses to give in to it.

"I'm so sorry, Kate," he says. "I'll be watching him all the time, you know. What can Jean and I do? Would you like me to call the girls for you?"

"Should I tell them to come?" she asks, with a break in her voice, afraid of what his answer will tell her.

"That's up to you. He doesn't need a respirator. That's a good sign. And the girls aren't far away, could get here pretty quickly if it came to that. Of course, they could probably be a big support to you, so it's your call. Come with me and I'll take you up to Coronary Care to see him."

Charlie is in Radiation when they get upstairs, but they have only been there a few minutes when he is wheeled into the CC on a gurney and moved into a bed. When he sees Katherine, he twists the right side of his mouth into a strange grimace and makes the same uhhhhhh sound as he did when they were at home. It takes her a minute to realize that he is trying to smile. She goes to him and kisses him, trying not to wince at the sight of his twisted face.

"I'm happy to see you too, darling," she says. But not like this, not like this, she thinks. She forces herself to smile back at him and squeezes his right hand and is pleased that he squeezes hers back. "You've had a stroke, Charlie," she tells him, "but Henry is taking care of you, and he thinks you have a good chance to get better. You have to stay in the hospital for a while, but I'll be here every day for as long as you want me." She pulls up a chair to his bedside and holds his hand. Henry tells Charlie that he is going up to look at his scan and will be back shortly.

When he returns, he sits down on the bed next to Charlie and speaks to him. "I'm afraid it is a stroke, Charlie, and we don't know right now exactly how serious it is. However, we do know that it's not a brain hemorrhage. The problem is a tiny blood clot that keeps a specific area of your brain from getting the blood and oxygen it needs. The good news it that it showed up clearly on the scan, and now we can give you medication that will break up the clot. You'll have to be here in the hospital for a while, and you'll need considerable therapy after that, but with some hard work on your part, and some luck, you'll recover a lot of your speech and motion. I'll look in on you later this evening."

He pats Kate's shoulder and says he will tell Jean what has happened. Then he leaves and she is alone with her husband.

It is a long afternoon. Nurses come and go, injecting shots into the I-V that was inserted as soon as he got to the emergency room. They draw several vials of blood. Above his bed a screen monitors his vital signs. She doesn't want Charlie to realize that she is watching his heart beat and his blood pressure rise and fall, but her eyes return again and again to the screen, and she feels her own heart race every time the rhythm of his cardiac line changes its pattern. At one point the nurses ask her to leave, and she goes to the cafeteria and has a sandwich and a cup of coffee. When she returns, she sees a tube from under his bed sheet to a jar on the floor and realizes they have inserted a catheter. She knows what an indignity this must have been to a proud man like her husband. At least, she thinks, Henry has arranged for him to have a private room in the CC.

Charlie falls in and out of sleep while she sits beside him, holding his hand. When he is awake she talks to him. At one point when he dozes off, she falls asleep herself, exhausted. When she wakes, his eyes are still closed. She takes his hand in hers again and puts her head down on the edge of his bed. They have been married for fifty years, and not since the war, WWII, has she thought of his dying. Now she can think of nothing else. "Oh, darling, don't leave me," she whispers. We're like two trees, she thinks, planted side by side as saplings. Now we've grown together, roots tangled with roots and branches with branches, impossible to take one down without destroying the other.

She begins to weep silently, blotting her eyes with the sheet so that her tears won't fall on his hand.

I'll have to be strong, she thinks. He's going to need me to be strong and to take care of him, and I can do that. I won't let him see how frightened I am for him. Oh, damn, why didn't I get that knee operation last year when Dr. Rite told me to. Now when I need two good legs, it's probably too late.

When Henry returns, Charlie wakes, and Kate rises quickly and turns away so that he won't see that she's been crying. Henry pats her on the shoulder and sits down on the bed next to Charlie and speaks to him.

"You look better already, more color for one thing. Those drugs you're getting are really miracle workers. A few years ago we just didn't have anything like that to treat stroke patients with. Now, Katie, I need to examine Charlie again, and I know how tired you must be, so you go on home, and you can come back to be with him tomorrow. Have you called the girls? Well, you'll want to now, and tell them for me that we have things under control here. Jean's already dropped off something for your dinner, and she says if you want her to come over, just call." And he all but pushes her out the door. As she walks down the hall, she can hear him saying, "Squeeze my hand with your right hand. Now your left."

When she gets home, the apartment is dark and unwelcoming. There are foil covered dishes on the kitchen table—Jean's dinner, she thinks, how can I eat? She knows she doesn't want to go to the dining room at the main building—all those explanations to make to concerned residents. She puts the food in the refrigerator and goes out to the living room to collapse on the sofa. The blinking phone indicates that there are eight messages waiting for her. Oh, lord, she says to herself, the news must be out. Damned if I'm returning any of those calls tonight.

Then she thinks of Lolly and Prill. Oh, dear, she sighs, I've got to call them before I go to bed. They'll be so mad at me if I don't. I just don't know how I can deal with the two of them and do whatever I need to do for Charlie. I've got a degree from a good college, and I've run this household and raised them—not always easy—and yet they can make me feel like an idiot within five minutes after they walk in the door. I'm proud that they've been so successful, and maybe they have to be tough in their jobs, but sometimes I wish they could just be satisfied with being boss at work and not boss me all the time. She sighs again and picks up the phone.

And it is just as she expected.

"Dad's had a stroke?" asks Prill. "Are you sure, Mom? Have you gotten a second opinion? I think he should go to Boston right away. They have a wonderful neurology department at Mass General. I know Henry Bell is an old friend and has Dad's best interests at heart, but he's just an internist, and he's getting pretty old himself. I'll find out who's the best neurologist at Mass General and call him about seeing Dad tomorrow afternoon. I think I can borrow the company plane to take him there. Don't worry about a thing."

"But I don't know if your Dad wants to go to Boston, Prill. Please don't do anything till you get here."

"It will be all right, Mom. I'll take care of everything." And she hangs up.

The conversation with Lolly isn't much better.

"Oh, Mom, how terrible. Poor Dad. He can't talk or walk or move his left hand? What an awful way for him to spend the rest of his life. Well, we can set things up so he's as comfortable as possible under the circumstances. We can take the table out of the dining room and put in a hospital bed and get one of those special vans that takes a wheelchair. Of course you can't take care of him by yourself, but I think your long term health insurance covers the cost of an attendant."

Kate feels anger and despair in equal proportion. She also feels assaulted. *I know I have to think about these things, but I can't do it yet. It's all so sudden. I'm too upset to think straight.*

"Mom? Are you there, Mom? I'll be down in the morning to see Dad and help with all the arrangements."

"Good-bye, Lolly," says Kate, but Lolly had already hung up.

Kate goes to the kitchen and takes two sleeping pills with a glass of milk and goes to her bedroom. The pills get her through the night, but when she wakes at seven and stumbles out of bed, they are still clouding her brain, and even after a hurried cup of coffee, she makes herself drive very carefully on her way to the hospital. She takes a deep breath before she enters Charlie's room, but when she sees him, she thinks she sees some slight improvement in his appearance. "Blah, blah, blah," he says, and for a moment she thinks he is making some kind of strange joke, but he frowns, and she realizes that he is unable to say what he wants to. In his frustration he hits the bed as hard as he can with his right hand. Katherine goes to his side and puts her face against his.

"I know it's terrible for you right now, my darling, but it's going to get better, I promise you. Henry says so, and he wouldn't if it weren't true."

She can feel him relax as she whispers to him and caresses him, but then she tells him the girls are coming today, and his body stiffens and he hits the bed again. She knows he does not want them to see him in his present state, so weak and helpless. I should have insisted that they give him a few days, she thinks, but when have I ever been able to stand up to them? Not since they were babies, and not always then.

Later her daughters arrive with the force of two jet streams blowing down from Canada. Prill, who has commandeered her company's plane, is the first to get there. She sweeps into Charlie's room wearing one of her office outfits, a handsome black suit with a Hermes scarf at her throat, her dark hair in a chic bob. Katherine, who has thrown on a pair of wool slacks and a sweater, which she now realizes has a grease spot on the front, feels like a scruffy teenager beside her. It doesn't help that Friday is the day she always has her hair done and right now it has reached its end-of-the-week condition, which means she looks, or thinks she does, like a bag lady. I need to call Jose and tell him I have to cancel, she reminds herself. And today he was going to cut it. Oh, dear, I'll be a mess all weekend. I wouldn't care if the girls weren't here, and God knows Charlie doesn't care, but I do hate having them see me at my worst.

She hugs her daughter, and then Prill breaks away and goes to Charlie's side. She kisses him on his forehead, then draws away and pats his arm gingerly.

"Oh, Dad, what a piece of bad luck. But I've got the name of a marvelous neurologist in Boston at Mass General, and I've got the company plane here to take you there. There's actually a fold-out bed on it, so you'll be perfectly comfortable. Everyone says this doctor is the best in the Northeast, and we all want you to have the best."

She has positioned herself a foot away from his bed, just out of his reach on his right side.

Why, she's afraid, thinks Katherine, not of him, but of his condition. She doesn't know how to deal with seeing her father so helpless. Katherine is indignant for him. Isn't it bad enough that he is stricken by this stroke? But she knows that Charlie is probably unaware of Prill's feeling. In fact, he is concentrating on making it clear that he does not want to go to Boston, will not go to Boston.

He hits the bed again, and Prill flinches. He tries to shake his head and does, not very effectively, but Katherine understands.

"Prill," she says. "I know your Dad is grateful, but he really doesn't want to go to Mass General. In the end the decision is up to your father."

Prill starts to protest. "But, Mother," she says, and gets no farther because at that moment Lolly arrives. She is wearing a soft blue wool dress and her blonde hair is in a severe chignon. She looks cool and collected as she always does, and she goes straight to her father, puts her cheek against his, and says, "Oh, Daddy, I'm so sorry. I'm here to help you and Mom. I called my staff and my Board last night, as soon as I heard, and they said I can take off for as long as I'm needed here." She stands beside him, holding his hand and caressing it.

Well, at least she's not afraid of his stroke, thinks Katherine. Prill, who is also watching Lolly's display of affection, bites her lip.

Kate watches as her two daughters stand side by side next to Charlie. They begin to talk to him about their jobs, and he looks intently at whichever one is speaking. They know he loves to hear about their work and is proud of their success. He likes to brag about them to his friends. They have often overheard him talking about them.

"Prill's president of a division of Meredian. It's one of the top three hotel chains in the country. Her division handles special events, conventions, business conferences and shows. It's a big job—she makes more in a year than I ever did. Lots of head hunters calling her, but she likes where she is, and they like her."

"Lolly? Yes, Lolly's still head of Windsor. Everyone says she's transformed that place. Always had a big reputation as one of the best prep schools in New England, but stuffy. Lolly's changed that. She's brought it up to date, added new courses, created study abroad programs, brought in resident artists. Now it gets more applications than any other school of its kind."

All true, and yet Katherine can't help but be aware that something is missing in her children's lives. None of Prill's relationships with men have been successful. At the beginning of each new affair, strong, invincible Prill softens, lets herself become vulnerable and falls in love with the same intensity that she brings to all the other aspects of her life. Invariably, she demands too much, and when her lover backs off, she is wounded beyond all reason. The romance falls apart, and Prill is left more isolated than ever. Although she is aware of the destructiveness of her behavior, she seems powerless to change it. Poor Prill, thinks Kate.

Lolly's early marriage ended in divorce. She shares custody of her two children with her former husband, but her relationship with him is contentious, and Katherine thinks her grandchildren, her precious grandchildren, suffer from being shuffled back and forth between their parents. Despite her outward composure, Lolly finds her job intensely stressful. She has told her parents that it is difficult to please so many constituencies: her board, the faculty, the students, the alumni and, perhaps hardest of all, the parents. Kate knows that Lolly, who never had much interest in clothing or any other aspect of her appearance, has transformed herself into this immaculate stylish woman because she believes that in her role as head of school, her presentation is important, but the effort to be all things to all people shows in the deep frown lines that appear and reappear on her forehead.

Katherine wants to feel about them as Charlie does. And she does in a way. Of course she is proud of their achievements, their beauty, their daunting intelligence. But these qualities do not draw them to her. Rather, she feels that they stand between her and her daughters. It is not exactly that they are cold, that they consciously push her away, but there is a certain coolness in their manner, in the dry kisses they brush on her cheeks in greeting, the phone calls they put off returning, the excuses they make for forgotten birthdays, the cell phones they allow to interrupt conversations with her. In their company, she feels diminished, less than she believes herself to be.

And she takes the blame for her failed relationships with them on herself. For always, when they were children, it was Charlie who was first in her heart, and, to be honest, he still is. "The love of my life," that's how she thinks of him. Not that she didn't love Prill and Lolly, such bright, pretty little girls, but as consuming as their need was for her, it was always Charlie whose needs came first. "Quiet, girls, Daddy's working on his lecture." "Go outside and play, you two, Daddy's writing his book." "I'm sorry I'll miss your play, but I need to be at the party for Daddy." The best part of each day was the hour after she had read them a story and tucked them away in their beds, when she could go downstairs and spend an hour playing Scrabble with Charlie and listen to the news of his day. I thought they would be more interesting when they got older, she thinks, and they were, but by then they had lost their desire or need for her attention.

She remembers the summers when they went off to camp. Early in the morning she and Charlie would drive them to a gathering place for the camp bus where milling parents and children waited for the campers' names to be called. For the first two years, Lolly was the youngest member of the group, probably too young for camp, but with Prill to accompany her, Kate rationalized that she would be happier at camp with her sister than at home without her. When it was their turn to board the bus, they kissed their parents goodbye, and with Prill holding Lolly's hand, they climbed on and took their seats. As the bus pulled away, Kate and Charlie smiled and waved to the two little figures with their small, sad faces pressed to the glass of the window as they solemnly waved back.

Some of the other parents were clearly fighting back tears as the bus turned out of sight, but Kate and Charlie couldn't repress their gleeful smiles as they ran for their car. Kate remembers thinking, "two months alone together" as they drove home. Laughing, they dashed up the stairs to their bedroom where they fell into their unmade bed. Oh, those beautiful summer days, she thinks, when we could make love without shutting the bedroom door, the warmth of the sun coming through the south windows on our bare skin. Charlie was home most days except for a few hours at the library and at his office at the college. Usually his research required a trip to France or Germany for two or three weeks, and they would go while the girls were at camp, and they could stretch their stay for a vacation together. She told herself the children loved camp and were better for the experience, more independent and resourceful. When they outgrew camp, they were eager to go to special programs abroad in the summer, and they took for granted the four years of boarding school. Of course, Kate tells herself, of course it was good for them to learn how to look out for themselves. Look what strong and successful women they've become. But I wish, I wish...I wish I'd enjoyed them as much as I enjoyed Charlie. I wish I'd had more fun with them.

And here they are, she and Charlie and their girls, all of them in this small square hospital room. How long has it been since they have been together like this? Not since Lolly's wedding, almost ten years ago, thinks Kate. She sees her daughters from time to time, of course—an occasional lunch in Boston with Prill, and Lolly sometimes comes with her children to spend Saturday night on one of those rare weekends when she has the children and no pressing duties at Windsor. But most weekends when other residents are surrounded with their visiting children and grandchildren, she and Charlie are alone. They are not as sociable as most of the other residents who make dates to eat dinner with their friends almost every night. Many nights they eat alone, enjoying each other's company as they always have. But sometimes on Sunday, Kate wishes they could have their family with them.

The day drags on. She and Prill and Lolly take turns sitting with Charlie, but the time seems endless. When she goes to the lounge or to the coffee shop with one of them, each daughter pushes her agenda. Prill continues to press for a second opinion from the Boston neurologist. Lolly has countless suggestions as to how Kate can rearrange the cottage at High Meadows to accommodate Charlie's new "disabilities." Both of them bring up old issues to discuss in the light of these recent events. For some time they have urged their parents to sell the summerhouse on the Cape they bought when the girls were in college.

"You won't be going there, Mom. Daddy's not up to it now, and he may never be."

"He won't be able to drive. Perhaps this is a good time to get rid of the Audi. You'll do fine with one car."

"Let us help you get someone to be with him when he gets home. You know you'll need help—he's too big for you to move or support, especially since you put off having that knee operation." She feels assaulted, under siege, and finally Lolly goes upstairs so that Prill can come down for a cup of tea.

But it is not Prill, but Henry, who comes into the cafeteria and sits down with her, taking her small hand in his large one.

"They're pushing you, aren't they, Katie?" he says. "I overheard them talking upstairs when Charlie was asleep. Nothing like children trying to run their parents' lives. Bobby keeps telling me it's time for me to retire, and he's right, it is. But I just don't want to let it all go. I love what I do, always have, but I have to admit I'm not as sharp as I used to be. Sometimes I forget things. Bobby wants me to give up driving, and I probably should. My reactions aren't as fast as they once were, and my ophthalmologist tells me I have the beginnings of macular degeneration. What kind of doctor would I be if I couldn't drive myself where I'm needed? So I'm planning to retire at the end of the year."

"Oh, Henry, what will Charlie and I do without you?" says Kate. "Especially now with Charlie as he is. But that's selfish of me. Of course you have to do what you feel is best. But I'll miss you being our doctor. We go back a long way."

"Yes, we do," says Henry. "You know, Kate, I heard what the girls want you to do, and I have to tell you, I think they're right. I'm an internist and I've treated a lot of folks with stroke, but if Jean had one, I'd want to take her to Mass General to Douglas Grant. He's about the best in the country. Charlie will improve a lot if he stays here, but he might do even better with Grant at Mass General. They have a great rehabilitation unit there. I wouldn't move him for a few days, but I'd get him there as soon as he's stable."

"But he doesn't want to go. He wants to stay here with you."

"Nevertheless. And I agree with Lolly that you're going to need some help when he gets home. Take my word for it—and don't find out for yourself the hard way. And frankly, I don't think he will be able to drive again, so you might want to think about selling his car and becoming the permanent designated driver. Also, your place at the Cape is not going to do any more—too many steep stairs. Charlie probably won't be able to go there this summer anyway. Even with successful physical therapy, I don't think he is going to be able to cope with those stairs. And for that matter, with that weak knee of yours, you shouldn't be trying to either. Maybe you should think of putting that house on the market. It doesn't sound like your girls want it."

Kate is aghast. "You—they—you're all lining up against us. It's hard enough to keep control of our lives without you going over to the enemy."

"But they're not the enemy, Kate. I see this happening with patients our age all the time. The generations are wrestling for control, and we old folks don't want to give it up. But our kids worry about us and think they know what's best for us, and sometimes they do, and so they try to direct our lives. It's happening with me and Bobby, and it's happening with you and Prill and Lolly. Your girls are young and strong and smart. Let them take some of the responsibility for Charlie. It won't be easy for you to do. You're no pushover. Where do you think those girls got all that strength and determination?" He leans over and kisses her on the cheek. "And that's all I'm going to say about that," he says as he turns to go back upstairs.

Katherine sits alone in a corner of the cafeteria. She feels as if her breath has been sucked out of her, taking with it her strength and her confidence. She is angry, angry at her daughters who seem to be usurping her right to be Charlie's caregiver, angry at Henry for agreeing with them. She starts to get up and go back to his room, but as she stands, her bad knee crumples, and she feels the usual sharp pain that accompanies it. She falls back heavily into her chair and takes a deep gasping breath. As she exhales and the pain slowly subsides, she realizes that her anger is fading as well. Perhaps I can't do it all alone, perhaps I will need help, she thinks. She begins to understand that she does not have to care for Charlie and joust with her daughters at the same time. Henry is right, they are on my side, she thinks. No, they and Charlie and I are all on the same side together. She feels that somehow Henry has given her permission to share the burden of this painful trial. Yes, we can do it. My brave, beautiful daughters will lend me their strength, she thinks, and we will come through this hard time together.

She takes out her compact and her lipstick and paints on a new face of courage and confidence, and goes back to join her family in Charlie's small square hospital room.

# Barbara and Tom

Barbara Dalton is driving her chocolate Lab, Bo, to the vet on a very cold February day. The country road is narrow. There are snow banks on either side and icy patches as well. She needs to concentrate on her driving, and Bo, as usual, is not helping. He is standing with his hind feet on the seat behind her and his front paws on her shoulders, trying to nuzzle her neck. Her headrest creates an obstacle, but he is persistent in his efforts to circumvent it. She can feel and smell his hot, unpleasant breath on her cheek, and she knows he is drooling copiously on the collar of her boiled wool jacket.

"Bo," she says to him in the loud firm voice she always uses when she is giving him an order. "Bo, stop that. Lie down. LIE DOWN!"

Reluctantly and awkwardly, he begins to obey. There is a scrabbling sound on the leather seat and his paws are removed from her shoulders, but now she can see his head in the rear view mirror. He is sitting on the seat, prepared to climb on her back again at the first opportunity.

"BO! YOU LIE DOWN. NOW!"

His head disappears from the mirror, and in a quick glance over her shoulder, she can see that he is stretched out on the back seat. He gives her a reproachful look and then closes his eyes and sleeps.

Barbara is very angry. Her husband Tom died just a month ago, and it feels as though her whole life has fallen apart, which, indeed, it has. Nothing is what it once seemed. She is alone, which is what she used to wish for, but not this way, she thinks, not this way. Her friends think she grieves for Tom, and she did, but no longer. Now she grieves for herself and her own life and for what it might have been. As she drives, she feels a great surge of anger, and she cries out and hits the steering wheel in her frustration. Bo wakes and takes her unfamiliar action as an invitation. He starts to rise, and she cries out at him, "Lie down, damn you, Bo. LIE DOWN!" He gives up and collapses back on the seat.

She and Tom always had dogs. The day after they returned to Boston from their wedding trip, they went to a kennel to buy a puppy, a golden retriever they named Honeymoon, which they shortened to Honey. She was a lovely dog, gentle and quiet—well, quiet after she got through puppyhood and adolescence. Barbara always associated her with those happy early years of marriage when she and Tom walked with her in the wooded parks of their Boston suburb, talking, talking, so interested in each other's dreams: Tom's plans for his own business, hers for the children they would have, the names they would give them, the schools they would go to, the wing they would add to their house. Tom, sooner than he had thought possible, did start his own business, one of the early high tech companies which he sold later for more money than either of them had ever imagined. But there were no children, would never be, and they had had to put aside those dreams. Barbara thought that giving up the hopes that she had had for them was hardest for her because Tom had his work that he found so absorbing. Now she wondered.

Honey lived a long time, almost fifteen years. She had filled a little of the vacuum in Barbara's life that children might have occupied, and Barbara tried to fill the rest with volunteer work. Mostly she worked at the local hospital, helping to run benefits and other money raising projects. After a few years, she was asked to head a capital fund drive to increase the hospital endowment, and her success led to an offer of a paid job as Director of Development, which, after consulting with Tom, she accepted. They had no need of the extra income, for Tom's company was already very successful, but without expressing it out loud, they each hoped that the recognition that went with a paid job would offset the feeling of failure that Barbara experienced whenever she thought of the children she could never have.

A few weeks after Honey died, Tom brought home a small black bear cub which he identified to Barbara as a Newfoundland puppy.

"But, Tom, how can I housebreak him or train him when I'm working full time?" asked Barbara, somewhat annoyed that he hadn't foreseen this problem.

"You don't need to worry about that." said Tom. "Mrs. Linsky can take care of him." Mrs. Linsky had been their housekeeper since Barbara began her work at the hospital.

But Mrs. Linsky did not like dogs and gave immediate notice when she learned that she would be expected to care for one. No matter. A Mrs. Manero was soon found to take her place, and she loved dogs and was happy to come early and work late in order to feed, train, housebreak and walk Smokie. They paid her handsomely for her services, but they never begrudged her large salary, for they both fell in love with this large, clumsy puppy and blessed Mrs. Manero for making it possible for them to keep him.

He grew in his first year to be as large as a fully grown bear. Bypassers on the street sidled to the edge of the sidewalk to let him pass when Tom walked him. Mothers clutched their children until he was past. No stranger, seeing him briefly, could imagine his true nature, for he was as gentle and timid as a new fawn. Tom came home laughing after a walk with him one Saturday afternoon. "What a baby," he said. "He was attacked by a small toy terrier who slipped his leash and came running at him, barking as though he were the Hound of the Baskervilles. His owner was terrified and kept screaming, "Baby, come back. He'll eat you." Meanwhile Smokie was cowering behind my legs, trembling so hard I could feel him right up to my shoulders. I said, "Madam, your ferocious dog is frightening mine. Will you please take him away?" And finally she darted forward, scooped up Baby, and spoke soothing words to him all the way down the street. He continued to bark and snarl at poor old Smokie over her shoulder until she carried him around the corner. Smokie may look like a bear, but he's really the Cowardly Lion."

Perhaps it was his fearfulness that made him special to them. At the first faint sound of thunder he would climb under their bed and moan. Heavy rain on the roof affected him similarly. The sight, or perhaps it was the sound, of a roaring tiger on the television screen, once sent him right up onto the sofa and into Barbara's lap. When Smokie cowered on the floor, terrified by wind rattling the window sashes, Tom would sometimes lie on the floor beside him with his arm over his body. Tom said he could hear Smokie's heart rate gradually return to normal

"Poor darling," said Barbara.

"Poor old fellow," said Tom.

The dog did sometimes seem to be the only thing that they could feel close about anymore. Tom was immersed in his business. He often left early for breakfast meetings and stayed late to entertain customers at dinner. He traveled a great deal too, often being out of town all week. Meanwhile Barbara was trying to learn the politics of her new job. She would have liked to consult with Tom and ask his advice, but he seemed to have very little interest in her work or time to give her. On weekends she asked him to take her dancing, something they were once good at and enjoyed, but he always put her off, citing special work projects he needed to complete. Although the cost of theater tickets they had struggled to afford in the earlier days of their marriage was now no problem, Tom no longer cared to go out. It seemed that they had no common interests any more, and the bonds of love that once held them together had loosened. Barbara felt that either of them could slip them at anytime.

One day at work Barbara had lunch with one of the Boston philanthropists whom she was trying to interest in making a gift to her hospital. He was an agreeable looking man whose wife had died about six months earlier, and Barbara could sense that he was lonely and that he found her attractive. She made it clear that she was married, he told her he was sorry, and that was the extent of their personal conversation. But that night in bed, she thought about him and about her own situation. She realized that she would live many more years—she was only forty-five—and that if her love for Tom, and presumably his for her, had faded to this present pale indifference, there was little point in continuing their marriage. It was a liberating thought, and one she found herself pursuing often in the following weeks. Strangely, she thought, she did not imagine life with another man, but rather life on her own, a chance to be whoever she could be without always having to move in lockstep, harnessed to another person. The freedom that she envisioned was so heady that she began to think about how she might explain to Tom that she wanted a divorce.

Then, before she made a decision, she went for her annual mammogram and found that she had breast cancer. A biopsy showed it to be a fast growing type, but it had not yet spread to her lymph glands. Her doctor recommended a radical mastectomy, and a second doctor concurred.

Tom was far more upset than she had imagined he would be. She even wondered if the doctors had given him a bleaker diagnosis than they had given her, although he assured her this was not the case. He was more tender than she had seen him in many years. She was terrified of the operation she was about to have, but he promised to be with her until she went into the operating room. "And I'll be there right beside you when you wake up," he told her.

"I'll be so ugly," she said. "all lopsided with a great red scar on my chest."

But he refused to listen. "No," he said. "Not to me. To me you'll always be that beautiful girl in the red dress that Henry Peters introduced me to at a New Year's Eve party in Scarsdale."

When she came home from the hospital, he changed his business habits so that he could spend more time with her. He rarely made trips out of town anymore, and when he did they were short ones. He came home every night to have dinner with her, and he gave up business breakfasts altogether.

Barbara began to feel that she had misjudged her husband. She decided that his previous indifference had simply been preoccupation with his growing business. Her own dissatisfaction with her marriage now seemed unjustified. He was certainly not unfeeling as she had thought. His care for her during her operation and the unpleasant radiation treatment that followed it surely demonstrated that he was a loving husband. She felt ashamed that she had wanted to abandon their marriage. How deeply he would have been hurt if I had asked for a divorce, she thought.

But when she was well enough to go back to work, some of her old doubts reemerged. She began to feel again the dissatisfaction with her life that she had felt before she was ill. She realized that she was happy to leave the house in the morning and that she delayed her homecoming at night as long as possible. And although Tom was physically present, he often seemed distracted by his own thoughts.

Perhaps she might have left him then, but she was deterred by the sudden death of Smokie. He was only eight years old when he developed a massive internal infection that antibiotics could not cure. Perhaps it had started earlier than they realized, but less than twenty-four hours after Barbara and Tom took him to the vet, he was dead. Why didn't I see sooner how sick he was, thought Barbara. If I had only gotten him to the vet earlier, he might not have died. Tom told her she shouldn't blame herself; he too had not realized how sick Smokie was. But Mrs. Manero, who loved the dog as much as they did, looked reproachfully at Barbara through reddened eyelids. It was clear that she believed that if Smokie had gotten sick on a weekday when she was there, he would still be alive. Losing Smokie was much more painful than putting Honey to sleep.

She said to Tom, "I guess we knew that Honey was old and her arthritis hurt her so much that I really felt we were doing the right thing. She gave us joy for a long time, and I think she was grateful to us for ending all the pain. But Smokie was still young, and he was so afraid of everything. He needed us to protect him, poor dear. He was terrified of the vet, and he trembled and whimpered all the way into the office. I hated to leave him there. I felt I was deserting him."

Tom patted her on the shoulder in an absent-minded way, and went into his home office to work. She knew that he had loved Smokie as much as she had and missed him just as much, but it was not his nature to express his feelings. She resented his detachment, and the old dreams of independence began to stir. "I could still do it," she told herself. "I could start my own business, be a fund raising consultant. I have contacts now from my hospital work. It might take time, but I have enough income from Aunt Lizzie's legacy to get me started. I'm good at this work. I know I am."

She made plans to tell Tom after Christmas, but just before the holidays, she found she had cancer again, this time in her neck. There was another operation, not so drastic as the first, followed by a long period of radiation and chemotherapy. She had never felt so ill. She couldn't eat, couldn't sleep, and lost weight until she was a walking skeleton. When her hair fell out and her skin became thin and mottled, she wept, no longer able to maintain the brave face she had worn like a mask. Once again, it was Tom's devotion that sustained her. He worked at home so that he could sit with her whenever she was awake. When she was well enough to listen, he read to her and brought videos of their favorite musicals for them to watch together. He even sang to her the risqué songs he had learned as a member of a singing group in college.

"I never heard that before," she told him when he sang one particularly rowdy lyric.

"Never thought you were old enough till now," he said.

Then one day when she had partly recovered, he brought her a new puppy. She knew at once that he had bought it to be her dog for it was a small poodle, the kind of lap dog he had never really liked. But he had understood that she needed just such a small puppy as this one who was already squirming against her in the bed, putting her head on Barbara's stomach, looking up at her with dark worshiping eyes.

All of their dogs had let it be known that although they loved both Tom and Barbara, they did not love them equally. Honey had chosen Barbara as her mistress. Tom was simply a nice man who lived in the house with them. Honey was quite willing to accept pats and scratching from him, but it was clear that her primary love was Barbara. She followed her around like a toddler. Barbara adored the dog but sometimes regretted that she could not even go to the bathroom without Honey scratching the door and crying to join her.

But Smokie made it plain that he was Tom's dog from the day he brought him home. He sat wherever Tom sat and put his tousled head on Tom's knee to be rubbed. When he was patted he appeared to be in a trance, but whenever Tom faltered he would lift his huge head and push it under Tom's hand for more. When Tom couldn't stand it any longer, he would order the dog in his firmest voice to lie down. Smokie reluctantly obeyed, but he crawled between Tom's legs and the chair he was sitting in and lay on his back, an enormous black furry invitation to disaster when Tom tried to stand up.

"I think he likes me," said Tom apologetically to Barbara one night, "because he's such a big baby. He thinks because I'm a man and bigger than you, I can protect him better from all those monsters he imagines out there about to devour him."

"Thank God," said Barbara. "He's a dear, but I certainly don't fancy him climbing on me the way he does on you."

After he died there was no dog for a few years because Barbara was too ill to cope with one. She lay in bed, weak from the aggressive cancer treatment, and when she was finally well enough to cradle him, the small white poodle (such a contrast to Smokie) lying quietly in her lap was more comfort than she could have imagined. "I'm going to call him Dandy," she told Tom.

Barbara's convalescence was long and wearisome. As it dragged on she realized that she would not be able to return to work. Her dependence on Tom made the thought of divorce so impractical that she resigned herself to a marriage that had become disappointing. She reminded herself that even in the worst of her illness, he had been there to care for her. That he sometimes seemed remote, without the zest for life that for her had always been one of his most attractive qualities, was understandable under the circumstances. "I don't think he could ever comprehend my wanting to leave him," she said to herself. "I need him now because I'm weak and don't seem to be getting stronger very fast, and he would be so lonely if I were to go. He's not made to live alone."

As she slowly got better, Barbara began to make a new kind of life for herself. She cultivated the women friends that she had mostly given up during the years she worked for the hospital. She joined a book club and a poets' group. She took bridge lessons, and at her doctor's suggestion, she began a yoga class. She tried not to think that these years, her fifties, were the time of her life when she might have built a successful career and achieved the independence that had once been important to her. Now she knew that would never happen. She had given up the dream of having children years earlier, and now, slowly and painfully, she gave up her ambition for freedom and personal success.

She and Tom settled into a life of mutual accommodation. If he had unfulfilled dreams, she did not know what they might be. To her it seemed that he had achieved the goals that he had set for himself long ago: to be an entrepreneur, to start a successful business and to make a comfortable fortune. He had a reputation as a man of good judgment and served on many boards of both business and charitable organizations. Was there something more that he might have desired in his life? Did the children they never had leave a hole in his heart as they did in hers? He had never seemed as eager to have children as she had been, but perhaps he had suppressed his desire so as to ease her feelings of inadequacy. It was a question she could not bring herself to ask him. And so they lived together like two fine horses in tandem, harnessed to the same carriage but always separated by the yoke that bound them.

During these years Dandy was a bright light in Barbara's daily life. She was a dog of sweet disposition and instinctive good manners. She always lay on the bed or the sofa beside Barbara with her head on her leg. She seemed to understand from the beginning that Barbara was not up to the role of "puppy's playmate," and never frisked under her feet or ran around her in circles. She paid very little attention to Tom, other than avoiding him and his large shoes that could easily have broken her back if he had accidentally stepped on her. She never barked when Tom was in the house, as if she were aware that he particularly disliked the yipping sounds of small dogs.

When Tom turned seventy, he began to think of giving up their house in Springfield and moving to a retirement community. He was in good health, but Barbara had never fully regained her strength and energy since her last bout of cancer. He thought she would be better off in a continuing care community where her life would be simpler and where health care was always at hand. He was familiar with High Meadows because it was not far away and several of their friends were living there. When he told Barbara that she would be allowed to keep her dog there, she reluctantly agreed to move.

Dandy was an old dog when the Daltons finally got to the top of the waiting list at High Meadows. Her new circumstances unsettled her, and she stayed close to Barbara in the apartment and was desolate when Barbara and Tom left her alone. Barbara had to stay with her almost constantly so that she wouldn't bark and disturb their neighbors.

"She's so old. We never should have expected her to make this move," Barbara said to Tom one evening, when for the third time that week, they had to turn down an invitation to join a group in the dining room. "We should have waited until she died."

"Then we might have been on the waiting list until *we* die," said Tom. "You got the apartment you wanted, and it may be another four years before one like it is available. We can always ask for tranquilizers."

"Oh Lord, we would be the perfect zombie couple."

"I meant for Dandy, not for us."

Although their first year there was complicated by Dandy's problems, the little dog gradually became accustomed to her new surroundings. But a year after they moved in, she became ill with an kidney disorder that the vet declared untreatable, and when she began to suffer unrelenting pain, Barbara reluctantly allowed her to be put down. She knew that Tom had never particularly cared for Dandy and did not miss her as she did. She was not his kind of dog, too small, too dainty. And so Barbara mourned her privately. "My last dog," she told herself. "We're too old to raise another one."

Both the Daltons found that they liked living at High Meadows more than they had expected. Without the responsibilities of a big house, Barbara's health continued to improve. They made new friends, Tom was soon asked to be on the Board of Trustees, and Barbara agreed to serve on the Library Committee. She became a member of a bridge foursome that met on Monday afternoons. Tom used their second bedroom as a study and spent many hours there working on some of the consulting work he was still doing.

Then one afternoon he came home from the village with a dog, a small, black Labrador retriever.

"You didn't even ask me," cried Barbara, as the small puppy ran excitedly around the living room, sliding awkwardly whenever he was on the hardwood floor, crawling under a chair to attack an electric cord, and finally crouching in a corner to pee. "Oh, my God, he's not even housetrained. How could you, Tom? He's much too young for us to deal with, and we're much too old for a new dog."

"Well," said Tom sheepishly, "I know that. But I ran into Pete Silverman in town. He was walking this puppy that he bought for his grandson, and it turns out the boy is allergic to dogs, and his mother gave him back to Pete."

"Then let Pete keep him."

"He would, but then his grandson couldn't come to see him, and Pete wouldn't even be allowed in the house where the grandson lives because the kid is so allergic that he can't even be around a person who has a dog."

"Still, you didn't have to take him."

"I know, but the truth is, Barbara, I miss having a dog, a real dog. I'll house train him myself. You won't have to do a thing, I promise."

Barbara was about to say no when the little dog ran over to her and put its paws on her knees. Without thinking she scooped him up and held him. He was not much larger than Dandy had been when he was full grown, and she liked the feel of him in her arms, as he stood up in her lap and licked her neck. She stroked his back and scratched behind his ears. "Precious little puppy," she crooned, and Tom knew she was hooked.

Tom thought he was living up to his promise to take care of the puppy, whom they named Beaumont and called Bo. Mostly he walked the dog several times a day. He changed the newspaper on the bathroom floor and fed Bo and kept his water bowl filled. But there were times when he wasn't there and the dog's outing fell to Barbara. And it was Barbara who got up in the night to comfort him when he cried because he was afraid in this strange new place. She sat on the floor next to the cardboard box that she had lined with an old blanket where he was supposed to sleep, and patted him until he stopped whimpering. She let him curl in her lap to sleep in the daytime. She thought it was funny that he seemed to have chosen her for his special human, but Tom was not amused. "What a dear, good little fellow," she said to the puppy when she petted him.

Then he hit adolescence, and everything changed. He grew to be huge, too big to sit in her lap and too rambunctious for her to walk on a leash. She couldn't control his habit of jumping on people. He was a clear and present danger to all the frail residents of High Meadows. Tom was strong enough to restrain him, and so he took over all the dog-walking. And since now that Bo was big and strong and needed all the exercise he could get, those walks became the highlight of his day. If Tom was out, he waited by the door for his return and begged for his outing as soon as the door opened. When they were in the apartment he sat beside Tom's chair with his head on his knee to be petted. He had changed his allegiance, and Barbara admitted to herself that however foolish it was, her nose was out of joint.

She knew it was silly for her to care. As he grew up, he developed traits that made him unpleasant to be around. He slobbered excessively, and when he shook his head, he flung globules of saliva in all directions. No matter how often he was bathed, his skin had an unpleasant odor, and medication and diet changes had no effect on his constant flatulence. He frequently lay on his side and licked his genitals with great smacking sounds. And when Barbara's friends came to play bridge, he crawled under the table and stuck his snout in their crotches until they learned to slap him away as soon as he approached.

I should be glad he prefers to be with Tom in his study, Barbara thought, but she had bonded with him when he was small and helpless, and now her feelings for him were mixed, not love-hate, she thought, more like love-disgust.

One January evening after dinner, Tom took Bo for his nightly walk. It had snowed earlier, and the paths at High Meadows were only partially cleared. Near the daffodil garden, Bo saw a squirrel and dashed after it. He ran around Tom, who, tangled in the leach as the dog circled him, lost his balance and fell heavily, hitting his head on the hard frozen ground. With Bo's leash still twisted about his legs, he lay unconscious on the path, the dog beside him.

When he had been gone an hour, Barbara became concerned and called the desk in the entrance hall of High Meadows and learned that no one had seen him come in. An emergency crew found him on the path near the daffodil garden. An ambulance was called, but Tom died as it was taking him to the hospital.

For four weeks Barbara has grieved for him. She has remembered all the happy time: the early days of their marriage when they made plans for their future together, his understanding and tenderness when they learned that she would never have children, his care when she was ill with cancer. Now she blames herself for the times when he had seemed distant. It's my fault, she thinks, because I was restless, because I wanted too much. I was ready to exchange his love for independence. I should have understood how demanding his job was, how hard he was working. She feels as though she had spoiled something that might have otherwise been perfect, and she cannot forgive herself.

And now their lawyer has called and requested certain papers that are in Tom's study. She has hardly been in this room since he died, but she realizes that it is necessary, if painful, to deal with these practicalities. She goes systematically through his desk, compiling the documents that her lawyer has asked for until she comes to a drawer that is locked. Searching in his bureau, she finds several sets of keys, and among them is one that opens the drawer. In it she finds a folder holding photos of his family, his parents and brother and sister. They are old prints that she has seen before. Some are snapshots of Tom at various ages, and also pictures of friends, many whom she can not remember. Some she knows are college friends that she has never met: a young man in uniform, his picture labeled "Bob, d. Anzio, 1944;" Tom and his college tennis partner, dressed to play; an older man, "Professor Alex;" a blonde woman in a faded Polaroid shot, her hand shielding her face from the sun, no label. Who was she? wondered Barbara.

These were obviously pictures of people who meant something to Tom, so who was she?

Then she sees, pushed to the back of the drawer, a small lacquered box, also locked with a tiny padlock, for which she can find no key, and so she pries it open with Tom's letter opener. Inside are a few letters, folded to fit the box. There is no return address on the envelopes, but the postmarks are all Boston except for the last which is San Antonio. Barbara pauses only a few seconds, then pries the box open with Tom's letter knife and takes out the letters and reads them.

*April 14, 1973*

*My Darling Tom, Of course, I understand. You would not be the man I love so much if you walked away from Barbara now. My heart goes out to both of you. I'm so glad you didn't say anything about us to her before she got this terrible news about the cancer.*

*If this is our last communication, and I think it must be, remember that I will love you forever. All my love, Carrie*

I know when that was, thinks Barbara, my first cancer. But who is Carrie? Numbed with the shock of all this letter implies, she feels that she is seeing her marriage with a new clarity. I thought his care for me then was because he loved me. Was it only guilt and pity that kept him by my side when I was so ill, she wonders.

The next letter said simply "YES, I WILL" in large bold letters. Then, posted less than a week later,

*June 10, 1976*

*My darling, I am so sorry, for Barbara, for you, and for me. How awful for her to have to face another operation and all that dreadful treatment afterwards. Truly my heart goes out to her.*

*I think this must be the end for us. Fate is obviously against our ever being together. I know that in your heart, regardless of your love for me,—I could never doubt that—you cherish Barbara in a different way. If she recovers from this episode, she may need your support for years. And I know that I must get on with my life as well. I love you and I want you, but I don't need you, not as she does.*

*Don't write me, don't call me. I will miss you the rest of my life. Good-bye, my dearest love, Carrie*

There are two more letters. So much for ending the affair, thinks Barbara bitterly.

*March 29, 1981*

*Last night Roger Gayle asked me to marry him, and I accepted. (I believe you know him—he says he used to see you at electronic shows and remembers you well.) He is a kind man, and he likes the outdoors almost as much as I do.*

*He has a job offer in San Antonio, and we will go there right after our wedding next month. It's just a family affair, but I don't think you would want to be there anyway.*

*I'm glad Barbara is feeling better, and from my heart, I wish you both the happiness you deserve. I hope I have your blessing. You will always be the love of my life, Tom. Devotedly, Carrie*

The last letter is from San Antonio two years later.

*Dear Tom,*

*I have debated for months now whether I should write this letter, but I think I owe it to you. Knowing how you grieved because you and Barbara could not have children, I simply can't withhold from you the knowledge that you have a son.*

*You remember that last meeting to say goodbye that you wanted, when we met in Marblehead, just for a drink, we said, but I think we both knew that there would be more than that. I didn't even know at the wedding two weeks later that I was pregnant, and when we got to Texas and I found out, there was just no turning back.*

*So now you know. He is lovely and healthy, and Roger adores him. No, Roger has no idea that he isn't his father, and I want to keep it that way. So please, my dear, don't answer this letter or come to see him or acknowledge him in any way. There are too many people who will suffer if you do. I just wanted you to know, that's all.*

*Oh, you should know this. Roger's father was named Thomas, and to please his mother, Roger wanted to name the baby after him. We call him Tommy. It made me uncomfortable at first, but I've gotten used to it.*

*Carrie*

Barbara sits at Tom's desk, feeling that her whole marriage has been a sham. All those years when I wanted my freedom, she thinks, all those years. But then what would I have done when I was so sick? How could I have lived without his care? "Trapped, both of us," she says out loud. Something black and ugly rises in her chest, spreading up into her throat. She can't catch her breath, is choking on her anger. She begins to weep noisily, rocking back and forth, her hand over her mouth to prevent old Mrs. Gray in the next apartment from hearing her and coming to see what's wrong.

Finally she stops crying and goes back to the old photographs, holds up the one of the young blonde woman, scrutinizes it for some clue that will give her an answer, but there is nothing, even in the background, to tell her when or where the picture was taken. It may not even be the writer of the letters. And she had his child, she thinks. Oh, how I longed for a child, his child, and she was the one to have it. How unfair. And she begins to sob again.

She does not sleep well until the early morning hours, and when she wakes, her grief and anger have hardened into resolve. She eats and dresses, feeds Bo and takes him out to her car. When they arrive at the veterinarian's, she drags him out of the car by his collar and into the office. He knows where he is and puts up his usual resistance, but she pulls him along anyway, and inside he crawls under her chair and cringes there until they are called into the examining room.

Dr. Wilde is a small man, but he easily lifts Bo onto the table, speaking to him in a reassuring voice. "All right, all right, fella, we're gonna fix your problem."

And then to Barbara, "What is Bo's problem today?"

"I've brought him in to you to have him put down," she answers, willing her voice to be strong.

Dr. Wilde is shocked.

"But Mrs. Dalton, he looks to be in good shape. He isn't sick or anything, is he?"

"Dr. Wilde, my husband died three weeks ago. I cannot care for Bo. I have had surgeries that have left my arms and shoulders weak. I can't walk him or control him, and I want him put down."

"That's much too a drastic solution, Mrs. Dalton. If you can't keep him, let me try to find another home for him. I'm sure I can."

"Yes, you probably can, but I suspect he will be returned to you in a very short time. He's not a pleasant dog to live with. See how he's drooling on your coat. No medication you've given him has helped with that or with the skin condition that causes him to smell so bad, or with his constant flatulence. And he has other bad habits as well. The residents at High Meadows dislike him intensely. I will not take him back there. He is an odious animal, and I want him put down today."

Dr. Wilde is clearly aghast. "But, but...," he stammers.

Barbara turns to go. At the door, she says over her shoulder to the astonished Dr. Wilde, "And he is also unfaithful."

She stumbles through the office and out to her car. The icy wind freezes the tears that fill her eyes and run down her cheeks. "Damn him, damn him," she swears under her breath as she slides under the steering wheel and starts the drive back to High Meadows.

# Flower Power

Of the single men at High Meadows, Bradley Bell MacPhearson is considered by far the most desirable dinner companion. Bradley has lost none of his charm or the social skills acquired in his career in the Diplomatic Corps. He is in good physical condition, and his mind is as sharp as it was twenty years ago. He is a handsome man for his age (seventy-nine) with fine youthful looking skin and bright blue eyes. There are a number of women residents who dream of a romance with Bradley MacPhearson. However, they dream in vain. Beneath Bradley's fine exterior there is an emotional void. He says and does all the right things, but he is only going through the motions. Every day that the sun rises, he hopes he will be gone before it sets.

He retired from the State Department eleven years ago, but after he left, an ugly land dispute between two small but critical nations began to escalate. Bradley had built his reputation on his skill as a mediator in similar situations. In this case, the US government did not wish to become officially involved, and the President suggested that the UN appoint a commission to mediate. Bradley, no longer a US diplomat, was asked to head it. For the next four years he commuted between Asia and the UN offices in New York. Finally a treaty, the best he believed possible, was negotiated and signed, but it left both parties dissatisfied, and Bradley had barely retired for the second time when the two countries commenced an extremely savage war. This outcome was hardly his fault, but he was left with the feeling that his career had ended in failure. He and his wife Faith decided to leave Washington and move into a retirement home in the New England area. Bradley wanted to be no more than an hour from the MacPhearsons' summer cottage on a lake in Massachusetts, and High Meadows met this requirement. They also chose High Meadows because it was in the town where Bradley went to college, and as an alumnus, he would have the privilege of using the library to research for the memoir he planned to write.

Bradley and Faith had purchased the cottage twenty-five years earlier as a summer place, a respite from Washington and all its formalities. They often used it when they were on home leave from a foreign country. It is isolated, and can be reached only by a rough two-mile dirt road through a heavily wooded area. The lake on which it is situated is small, hardly more than a large pond, and there are only two other cabins on it, both hidden from view by the trees that overhang the shore. The three cabin owners arrange every year for the lake to be stocked with trout, and Bradley spends many hours in his canoe fishing the waters of Lake Mikiwanna. He has some misgivings about going into a retirement home at his age, but Faith is not strong and he is doing it for her. After all, he thinks, we can spend the warm months at the cottage.

But the most important reason that the MacPhearsons retired to High Meadows is that it is less than fifty miles from each of Bradley's siblings. He is the youngest of four children who are unusually devoted to one another. They write and phone each other at least once a week, and they visit as often as possible. After so many years of being in Washington and abroad, Bradley is pleased to be where he can see them more often.

On their first evening at High Meadows, Bradley and Faith find that the Welcoming Committee has arranged for them to have drinks and dinner with four other residents. Faith is pleased, but Bradley feels like a small boy whose mother has set up a play date for him with an unknown child. However, he knows enough to submit graciously. And he finds that he actually enjoys their new companions, a retired general and his wife, and another couple who were once well known travelers and explorers. They have been all over the world, and his articles and her photographs once appeared in a wide variety of publications. The conversation is lively and cosmopolitan. Everyone at the table has stories to tell of exotic lands and strange adventures. Bradley begins to feel that living here may not be so bad after all. When they leave the table, the General says to Bradley in a quiet aside as if he's been reading his mind, "You'll probably like this place more than you imagine. For the most part, people aren't intrusive. There's plenty of company when you want it, but you can always withdraw and be by yourself when you get tired of too much togetherness. You mentioned a book you want to write. There'll be time for that. I'm working on my memoirs, mostly my experiences in WWII, and I find long periods of peace during the day and a dinner hour with interesting conversation the perfect schedule for making progress on it." Bradley sees that this life style could work for him too, and gradually he and Faith settle gracefully into their new community.

In July they go to their lake cottage. One afternoon they are sitting on a deck that overlooks the lake. Bradley is reading a book, and Faith is working on her latest quilt. Suddenly she calls his name. He is just beginning a difficult paragraph and, not catching the urgency in her voice, continues to read until he finishes it. When he raises his head, he sees at once that something is terribly wrong. Faith has dropped her quilt and has one hand on the side of her head. She seems unable to speak and to be in pain. He rises and goes to her as fast as he can, but before he reaches her side, she slumps in her chair. At the hospital, the doctor diagnoses a massive cerebral hemorrhage, and tells Bradley that she will not come out of her coma. Two days later, Bradley asks for her respirator to be removed. "Nothing you could have done when she had the hemorrhage would have made any difference," the doctor assures him, but he knows that had he looked up when she first called his name, he could have held her in those last few seconds of her conscious life. He can not forgive himself.

The burial service is private with only his siblings present. He is ragged with grief and self reproach, but his sister, Sally, and his brother, Robert, stand on either side of him, and both take a hand and steady him with their presence. They brace him with their bodies. He can almost feel their care for him flowing up his arms from their hearts to his. They are all I have now that Faith is gone, he thinks. He is surer than ever that he did the right thing when he moved back to his roots and his family in New England.

He is also glad that he chose to live at High Meadows while Faith was still alive. He moved there because he believed that it would be a secure place for her if anything happened to him. They have never had children, and he wanted a home for her where she would be safe if she were completely alone. Now it is he who is alone, and he realizes that he is supremely unsuited to living by himself. Aside from the grief he is suffering from the loss of his wife of almost fifty years, there are pragmatic considerations. Living most of his life in countries where servants were abundant, he has never learned the practical skills necessary to run a household. He cannot wash or mend his clothes or clean a house. He has no idea how to cook. Even something as simple as frying an egg is more than he can manage. Shopping in a super market is totally beyond him. Fortunately the staff at High Meadows can handle all of these chores for him.

But there is no one who can assuage his grief for Faith. Perhaps because they had no children, they were especially close. Faith was a small quiet person. She was not his intellectual equal, and they did not discuss the ideas that interested him. But they both loved music and listened to it together for hours. Bradley loved to see her face light up when a symphony or opera came to a part she particularly liked. She had become an expert on arts and crafts and was sometimes asked to judge at juried shows. Her quilts, inspired by the folklore of countries where he was posted, had won prizes and were in great demand. He was proud of her and loved her more than he realized, and now she is gone. He can't get used to her not being there.

He is grateful to his siblings who are united in their efforts to help him through his grief. They call him almost every day, send him funny cards and clippings they think will interest him, and at least one of them drives over to see him every weekend or invites him to visit. Sometimes they all meet for a few days at the big house in Great Barrington, where they grew up and where Harry, a life long bachelor still lives with their long divorced sister, Sally. These are jolly occasions. They recall their life growing up together, their childhood escapades, their old beaus and girlfriends, the eccentricities of their mother and the boyishness of their father.

"Remember how Dad used to love our birthday parties? I think he used to plan his whole business schedule around them."

"He always came home early from the office and brought a present. And he sat at the table with our friends as if he were a kid too, and sang "Happy Birthday" and ate cake."

"Mother really didn't like his being there. I think she thought he was horning in on her territory."

"Yes, that's why she stayed in the kitchen—she was pouting."

Much laughter over this old reminiscence that has been resurrected many times before.

"He gave me a watch on my sixth birthday—just a cheap one as befitted my age—but I thought it was worth at least a million dollars," says Bradley.

"And you dropped it down the toilet by mistake the very next day," says his sister Sally, still sounding a little indignant that she hadn't got her first watch until she was eight.

"And when Daddy asked you where it was, you told him a bird came in your window and flew away with it." This from his one year older, almost twin, Robert.

Hoots and catcalls from his siblings.

"Hey, it sounded reasonable at the time."

"And Dad really walloped you. He said it wasn't for losing the watch but for lying about it," says Harry, the senior member of the clan.

"Oh Lord, I was so humiliated. Dad was so righteous. He could make me feel like a bug just by looking at me. But I learned one thing from that episode—if you're going to tell a lie, make it a good one."

"That's probably why you were such a good diplomat," says Harry, and Bradley laughs with the rest and points his finger at Harry and pretends to shoot.

They can go on with these old family stories for hours, and they often do. Except in their sequence, they never vary. However different the early tellings may have been, now there is one standard version of each. Bradley can tell the tale of Harry's painting his mother's antique chair and the ruckus that ensued, although he was not even born at the time.

Driving home from one such gathering, Bradley wonders just why there is so much comfort in the telling and retelling of these tales. Faith, and Robert's wife, Sue, when they were alive, found them tiresome and used to withdraw to another room. But for the MacPhearson siblings, they can never be repeated too often. Perhaps they take us back to a time when we were small, he muses, and our parents were there to make us feel safe. Wars and death and cruelty, all banished by them from that home. The stories of those days bring back that feeling of security, which, God knows, we all need at this time in our lives. Then he realizes that he is smiling and humming to himself. It has been over a year since Faith's death, and he can tell he is beginning to heal. "You were the best thing in my life, Faith. I'll never forget you."

There are tears in his eyes, but he knows they are tears of sadness, not the despair he has lived with for the last twelve months.

Back in his apartment at High Meadows, Bradley has just returned from dinner to his apartment, when his phone rings. It is his brother Robert, and Bradley starts to make some light remark of greeting when he realizes Robert is crying. He is weeping so uncontrollably that he can hardly speak, but finally manages to gasp, "It's Harry, Bradley. He went out to get milk for supper and ran off the road on the way into town and hit a rock outcropping. He was dead before the ambulance could get him to the hospital. We'll talk later about arrangements. I'm sorry—right now I have to let Sally know. He had my name in his wallet as next of kin, and I told them I'd call her."

"No," says Bradley, "I'll do that. I'll call you in the morning—early. I don't think any of us will sleep very well tonight. We can make plans tomorrow."

He hangs up and dials Sally's number. Sally has a volatile personality, and he has no idea what her reaction to this news will be. She has always been close to Harry, and especially so since her divorce twenty years earlier. But when he tells her what has happened, there is no outcry, only stunned silence. "Are you there? he says.

"Of course I'm here," she answers. "How could he do such a stupid thing—drive off the road like that? It's not even winter, no ice, no snow. I told him to forget the milk. Oh, damn, damn, damn!"

Bradley knows she is building a wall of anger to protect herself from her unbearable grief. "I'm so sorry, Sally," he says, and hears her burst into tears. She cries in long choking sobs, and he knows that nothing he says will comfort her. He realizes he can't get off the phone while she is in this state.

"Sally, Sally," he says, almost shouting her name, trying to break though her sobs. "Would you like me to come there and be with you tonight?"

He loves Sally dearly, but he has never learned how to cope with her contrary nature and her fierce rages.

She begins to cry more softly. Finally she says, "I want you to come, but it's late, and I'll worry about you all the time you're on the road. But Bradley, come in the morning, please."

He assures her he will be there by eight, and sinks back in his chair. Only now can he contemplate what the loss of Harry means to him. He sits on the couch and covers his face with his hands and weeps for the brother who was his hero when he was a little boy and has been a dear friend all his life. He weeps for the memories of the experiences they shared, all the dearer because they *were* shared, now his alone. He looks into the future and sees the relentless attrition of his family.

At the funeral, seated with Robert and Sally, he surveys his brother and sister and tries to imagine what their loss would mean to him. Robert, closer to him than any other person on earth now that Faith is gone, his constant playmate when they were children because of their closeness in age, his friend during the precarious years of adolescence, the one person among all the others, who has known all his weaknesses and failures, those flaws that he has tried to keep hidden from all the rest, even Faith—how can he bear life when Robert is no longer there to bolster his courage? It was Robert who recognized the dejection that he managed to hide from everyone else when his UN mission failed and urged him to write his book.

And Sally, the four years older sister, who bullied and teased and tattled on him and Robert when they were children, the tyrant that they feared and hated until they were teenagers. Then Sally went off to college and returned at Christmas with a new persona. She actually seemed to enjoy their company. It never occurred to them that they, too, now both in high school, had changed as well. She willingly drove them to the movies and went in with them to see the show. She taught them to play bridge, and when a young man from Yale came to visit, they all four played together. She still had a sharp wit that could be cutting, but she had become part of their team. Now time has softened the edges of that wit, and although she sometimes loses the temper that she has tried so hard to leash, her love for her two younger brothers is a constant in her life. And in mine, thinks Bradley.

He tries to listen to the words of the service. "The days of man are as blades of grass that are cut down in a moment," the minister intones. Bradley hears the words and he thinks, yes, it is true. In only a few more years, all of us, all who lived in that big old house in Great Barrington will be gone. After the burial, he stays with Sally for a fortnight, so that he can help her sort through Harry's possessions. It is a painful task for both of them.

When he returns to High Meadows, he falls back into the routine of his life there. Now the General is also a widower, his wife having died a few months earlier, and he and Bradley have become good friends. They are lonely men, although neither reveals much of his personal life to the other, but both are veterans of WWII, and they can talk for hours about their war experiences. The General was an officer with an armored division in Africa that went on to Anzio and then fought its way up the boot of Italy. Bradley was a young lieutenant, a forward observer with a division that was active in the Normandy campaign, the Hurtgen Forrest, and The Battle of the Bulge. Every day they are in the habit of walking several laps together on the walking path around the property, and both are in demand as dinner partners. Bradley is surprised when the General remarries eight months after his wife's death. He recommends that Bradley follow his example. "The world goes two by two," he tells him, but although Bradley likes women, he feels his heart is locked in a steel cage.

The decimation of his family continues. Less than a year after Harry's death, Sally calls to say she has advanced breast cancer, and her children are insisting that she come to Cincinnati where they both live and where they can take care of her. Bradley sees her only once before they whisk her away, and, although they talk on the phone frequently during the few weeks until her death, he does not see her again. Then Robert, his beloved almost-twin, tells him that his doctor, seeking the cause of Robert's vision problem, has found an inoperable brain tumor. He will not live more than a few months.

When his brother dies, Bradley knows that he is finally alone, the only remaining member of his large family, the single repository of all the memories they shared. At High Meadows, he keeps his grief to himself, a dark weight pressing on his heart. Only the General senses how much he is suffering and understands how difficult it is for Bradley to speak of his losses. And so they talk of the war and their own near-death experiences when they were young soldiers.

The General makes himself available every day. The two men walk together and play chess together. The General's new wife often invites him to have dinner with them and includes one of the attractive widows of whom there are many at High Meadows. She, too, obviously believes that the world goes two by two.

One day in October, the General invites Bradley to an Air Force show at a nearby base. At the end there is a fly-over formation that soars directly above the crowd. One by one the planes peel off and disappear into the clouds until there is only one left, a small speck in the distance, soon invisible. He follows the last plane until he can no longer see it, and tears spring to his eyes. He turns away so that the General cannot see his face. On the way back to the car, the General claps his hand on Bradley's shoulder; the gesture is the closest he has come to expressing the sympathy he feels for his friend.

All through the long winter, the longest Bradley remembers, he takes a daily walk around the property. Usually the General is with him, but sometimes he walks by himself. This exercise in the cold New England air is giving him some kind of respite from his grief. He has been hammered by fate and survived. He has lost all his closest lifelong companions, and there are none left to leave him. He believes that the future can hold nothing as painful as what he has already experienced.

The harsh winter is followed by an early spring. One day in late April, a particularly balmy day, he is walking the path alone, and he stops to sit down on what has become known as "the daffodil bench."

The daffodils planted there by a dying resident for his wife have spread over a large area, and they are at the height of their glory on this day. No one is able to walk the path without stopping to admire them, and Bradley, succumbing to their spell, interrupts his routine to absorb their beauty. And as he sits and looks at the scene before him, the little pond and the former pastures with the bright flowers all about, he feels the heaviness that has weighed him down for so long lifting.

He feels almost light hearted. Why now? Why today? he asks himself, and then he remembers another day almost sixty years earlier.

He was in Germany, west of the Rhine, his battalion having been pulled back across the river. His artillery battalion was set up in firing position in a pasture, and he was sitting under a tree about a hundred yards away, writing letters to his family and to Faith. At the base of a nearby tree, he could see a clump of daffodils, yellow and white, and beyond them, a landscape of green meadows and pale brown cows. So beautiful, he thought, an oasis of peace here in the midst of war.

He heard one of the men at the battery call to him, "Orders to move out, sir," and he groaned to think that he was going back to the front.

"Back across the Rhine?" he called.

"No, sir. Toward Paris. We're pulling out for good."

It came to him then that *his* war was over. I'm going to live, he thought. I'm going home. I'll see my family. I'll go back to school and get my diploma and marry Faith. I have a future! Oh, how glorious to have a future! He looked at the daffodils, and it seemed to him that they embodied all the hope he felt at that moment.

Now, almost sixty years later, daffodils on a hillside in New England are giving him the same message. "You have survived all these painful losses because you still have a future. *Carpe Diem.*" He thinks then of the General and how he had said "the world goes two by two," and he thinks of all the gentle widows who have leaned forward at the dinner table to catch his every word. And when he resumes his walk, there is a spring to his step that does not go unnoticed by the single ladies that he passes along the way.

# OTHER STORIES

# Last Leave

In March 1944, Peter Alsop, 2<sup>nd</sup> Lieutenant, Field Artillery, United States Army, was given a very welcome three day pass from his post at Fort Bragg, North Carolina. He was sure that this would be his last leave before going overseas; there were clear indications that his division was about to move out. Security required that he keep such thoughts to himself, and this was hard because there were sentiments that he would like to express to his parents when he was home, but even to hint at them would be a breach of military security.

Spring was already in full sway in North Carolina, and he watched from the train window as the season reversed to winter again. He was just past his twenty-first birthday, and until he went off to Officers' Candidate School at Fort Sill, he had never been further from New York than Princeton. Youngest child and only son, he had been coddled—he was the first to say so—by his parents and his two much older sisters. The support he had received in such abundance had fostered his self confidence in most ways, but it did not seem to help him in the one where he presently needed it most. He was about to go into combat, and he was deathly afraid. He knew, of course, that other soldiers were also afraid—how could they not be?—but it was his own fear that he had to deal with, and he was beginning to doubt that he could. He was good at his job, he knew. No one in his class at OCS could outshoot him when it came to directing the fire of artillery pieces, but what if his fear of death or terrible wounds paralyzed his will when it was most needed? He did not think of himself as particularly brave, and now he doubted that he could be brave enough when he was put to the ultimate test.

When he arrived in New York City, he walked into blustery winds, gray skies, and low temperatures. His parents, who had taken to spending the cold months in the city rather than at their large, hard-to-heat house on Long Island, were at the station to greet him and swept him off to their small comfortable apartment. Their joy at seeing him was palpable. They had planned a weekend of his favorite activities, and that night they took him out to dinner and to the theater. The next morning he slept until ten, then went off with his Dad to have lunch at the Yale Club, and later his Mother joined them for a matinee. He was aware that they were watching him closely for some sign of what the future held, but he knew they would not ask any direct questions, and he tried to give nothing away. He would have been uncomfortable with the intensity of their love if he had not experienced it always. As it was, he accepted it as a fact of his life. However, it made it all the harder for him to act as though this occasion were no different from any of many other meals and theater outings the three of them had shared together in the past.

That night was a Saturday, and because his Mother had mentioned to her sister, Phoebe, that he would be there, and she had told someone else—he was never sure how the news got to the Kembles—he was invited to a dinner party they were giving for their son Bob and his fiancee. Bob Kemble had been a classmate at Princeton, but Peter had not known him well, and he had never met his fiancee. Nevertheless Peter looked forward to the evening as a last chance to experience a social occasion like those of his pre-army days. With luck some of his other friends might be there.

However, when he arrived at the Twenty One Club, it was evident that this was the kind of patchwork party that occurred commonly during the war. Mr. And Mrs. Kemball wanted to have a party of their son's friends to meet his fiancee, but most of those friends were scattered around the globe, and so they had garnered any young people available, no matter how slim the connection. There was Kay Kemble, Bob' sister and her roommate up from Sweetbriar for the occasion, and a dashing Navy Lieutenant who had gone to St. Paul's with Bob and didn't seem to know him any better than Peter did. There was a young enlisted man who turned out to be Bob's first cousin from Boston, currently stationed at Camp Kilmer, a Vassar senior who spent summers at the same Jersey shore town as the Kembles, and Reg Williamson, whom Peter recognized from Princeton and who he remembered had roomed with Bob during freshman year before they had some kind of major falling out. Another half dozen or so young men and women made up the rest of the disparate gathering.

It might not have been the group that the Kembles would have invited under normal circumstances, but they were all young, and they all wanted very much to forget the war and have a good time. Peter congratulated Bob and met his fiancee whose name was Sarah but was "always called Sally," she said, and he told her some nice story about Bob on campus which obviously pleased both of them. He had a brief conversation with Bob's young cousin about his army experiences, which were few because he had only just finished basic training, and he listened to the Vassar senior describe her thesis which was in his own major, economics, and might have been interesting to him under different circumstances. By then he had worked his way around the room to Fay Kemble's roommate who had been his objective all along.

He had noticed her across the room when he came in, and he was pleased to see that she was also aware of him, because she turned to Fay Kemble who was standing next to her and asked her something, and Fay looked at him before she answered. Even from a distance of twenty-five feet he thought she was striking, and that impression was confirmed when he stood in front of her. She had eyes of a most unusual blue, the brightest blue he had ever seen, and features that were both sharply defined and delicate. But what was truly unique was her hair style, for at a time when fluffy curls and pompadoured page-boys ruled the day, her straight dark hair was cut shoulder length with long bangs to just above her eyebrows. It was as simple as a child's haircut and at the same time extremely sophisticated, and to Peter her appearance seemed so exotic that he wondered for a moment if perhaps she was a foreigner, one of the many refugees presently studying in American colleges during the war. However, this notion proved to be obviously mistaken when she spoke, revealing a slightly Southern accent.

"I'm glad you finally got here," she said. "I've been waiting for you." He wasn't used to such directness, and it confirmed his feeling that she was different from the girls he had known up to now. He hardly knew how to respond, and he suddenly felt shy.

"But how did you know I would be here?' he asked.

"I mean I'm glad you got over here to this side of the room," she laughed. "I saw you looking at me when you came in."

"I saw you looking at me too," he said. "I'm Peter Alsop. Bob and I graduated together from Princeton last May."

"I know," she said, "I asked. I'm 'Ma-rye-uh' Goodwell. Maria is spelled like Maria but the Virginia way is to say it to rhyme with papaya. You can imagine I've spent my life explaining that, especially in all those Catholic countries we've lived in. And now I live in Maryland, the original Catholic state, and, of course, nobody there says it right either. I've told my parents that if they wanted to give me a name that nobody but Virginians can pronounce that we should have just stayed in Virginia."

"Who's Papaya?" said Peter, totally confused.

She looked at him to see if he was joking, then laughed out loud.

"It's not a who, it's a what. It's a fruit, a tropical fruit. We used to eat them in Martinique—delicious!"

By this time he was beginning to feel not only confused but foolish as well. But then she put her arm through his and drew him to the table where dinner was about to be served. The engaged couple were seated at one end of the long table and the senior Kembles at the other, and beyond that there seemed to be no formal seating arrangement, probably due to the uncertainty of just who would be able to show up in these doubtful times. In fact Peter saw the waiters quietly remove two or three table settings and readjust the others accordingly.

"Oh, we must sit together," she said. "I've been counting on it."

Her presumption pleased him inordinately. She can't think I'm a total fool if she wants me to be her dinner partner, he thought.

On Maria's right at the table was a dashing young man in the uniform of the Free French Forces who was on temporary assignment in Manhattan and who had been asked to escort the daughter of friends of the Kembles. On Peter's other side was the Vassar senior he had already met. Maria turned to introduce herself to the French officer, and Peter was dismayed and impressed to hear her address him in his own language. The effect on the officer was electric. He immediately began a long, and to Peter, unintelligible speech which was the beginning of a dialogue with Maria that lasted through the first two courses. With no alternative, he turned to the Vassar senior on this other side, whose name he was never to remember, and started to talk with her. She was from somewhere in Westchester County and knew some of his schoolmates from St. Paul's, including two of his classmates, who, she said, had both asked her to the senior dance at the end of the year.

"Who did you go with?" he asked politely, not really caring and feeling frustrated that he could not even eavesdrop on the conversation on his left which was continuing in rapid French.

"Well, of course, I couldn't go with either," she said, "because neither of them knew about the other, and I didn't want them to find out."

Then she launched into a long story involving one of the two boys and a boathouse and a parrot with a pornographic vocabulary. Peter listened with half an ear, conscious all the time of Maria on his other side, breathing the scent of her perfume and feeling the pressure of her shoulder against his when she shifted her position to make room for the waiter to serve her. But she showed no sign of ending her conversation with the Frenchman, and so he forced himself to attend to his other dining partner and found himself enjoying her story in spite of his frustration.

"So," she concluded, "that was the end of Wally and me. I was just so mad with him, I wouldn't see him or go out with him for the rest of the summer. Seems silly now to have been so mean and stubborn about something so unimportant. He went into the Navy Air Corps that fall, and he got shot down somewhere in the Pacific last month. Did you know about that?"

Peter hadn't known, and the amusement he had felt at her story quickly faded. He had so far during the evening been able to banish thoughts of his fears for his own future, and the news of Wally's death brought them rushing back. His pleasure at the party, the good food, the wine, the pretty girls on either side of him whose perfume hung in the air around him dissolved into despair. At that moment, as if sensing his change of mood, Maria turned to him and whispered, "I'm so sorry. I want to talk to you so much, but this soldier can barely speak English and he hasn't been with anyone who can understand him in weeks. He's from Provence where my family used to go for the summer when we lived in France. He hasn't been home in years and all he wants to do is talk about Provence and his family there. Listening is my personal war effort. But you and I will be together after the party, won't we? And we can talk then."

This was good news. He had planned to ask her to go out with him later; at least he had before she had become so attentive to the Frenchman. But now he saw that she was only being kind to someone for whom she felt sorry, and without his even suggesting it, she expected to be with him after the party. He began to make plans for the rest of the evening—some place where they could dance and where they could also talk. He wanted to learn more about the life of this unusual girl who had lived in Martinique and France and spoke French like a French woman. He understood his Vassar tablemate—she had lived in the same kind of bedroom community as he, had gone to the same kinds of schools, probably attended the same kind of dancing classes. He was sure he could play "do you know?" with her and discover a whole network of common acquaintances. And there was a certain comfort in this commonality—he knew how to play the game with her. But there was excitement in difference and a certain mystery as well, and therein, he thought, lay the attraction of Maria.

About this time the guests began to rise with toasts to the engaged couple. There were several old friends whose little speeches sounded as though real thought and sincerity had gone into them. Bob's sister rose and in a trembling voice spoke sweetly of the important role her brother had played in her life and welcomed her new sister into the family. Toward the end Mr. Kemble gave a toast that was distinguished both by its lack of originality and its deeply felt sincerity, and then Reg toasted his fiancee so tenderly that she was moved to tears.

Then it was over—but no—for now Reg Williamson stood up on unsteady feet and, with his diction slurred by the wine and champagne and the cocktails before dinner, began to reminisce uncertainly about his Princeton days with Bob. He managed to tell several stories about escapades involving the two of them, some actually quite amusing, but then he began to ramble, and Peter could see from the look of concern on Bob's face and the elder Kembles' expressions of alarm that a diversion was needed. He rose to his feet and called for the Princetonians present to give a rendition of "Old Nassau", without which, he proclaimed in a voice more confident than he felt, "no occasion such as this one is complete."

To his relief Bob rose immediately to his feet, as did Mr. Kemble and a stranger at the far side of the table, and Reg after a moment of bewilderment straightened up and focused on Peter, and the five of them gave a spirited version of the Princeton song with all the usual arm waving that accompanies it. Their performance brought cheers and applause from the other guests and a grateful look from Mr. Kemble to Peter. But his real reward was a squeeze of his arm, a dazzling smile, and a sotto voice "well done" from Maria. Mrs. Kemble rose to her feet, a signal that the party was over, and after thanks and good-byes, Peter and Maria fled the room and were at last alone together on the streets of Manhattan.

They walked down Fifth Avenue in the direction of the Hotel Cromwell where a well known swing band played every night in the penthouse supper club. There, when the orchestra played they danced, and when it took a break, they sat side by side on a red velvet banquette and talked. Peter told her about his parents and his sisters, his schools, his summers swimming in the surf and sailing on the Sound, his love of theater and music. He spoke of his interest in politics and history. He told her of his plans to go to law school and to eventually join his father's firm in the city, although when he spoke of a future that he feared he might never know, he felt the old despair come flooding back.

When the band began to play again, they went back to the crowded dance floor where couples could do little more than stake out tiny territories and sway back and forth to the music. Many of the men were in uniform, and they held their partners tightly and stared above their heads with sad eyes. Maria's silky hair brushed against Peter's cheek. Why have I not met you until now, he thought. I should have known you two years ago when I could have asked you for a football weekend. I would have pinned a giant yellow chrysanthemum on your coat, and we would have sat side by side at the stadium where the only struggle to be won was a game. I wish you had been with me at the shore last summer. We would have walked the beach, and I would have taught you to ride the waves, and sailed with you on the Sound. He felt a terrible nostalgia for all that was past and a deep sadness for what had not been and might never be, and it was almost more than he could bear.

Back at their table, she began to tell him about herself. She was born in Algiers where her father had been posted in his early days as a Foreign Service Officer. Later he had been sent to Paris where her younger brother was born, and the family had lived there for several years. Her mother, she told him, had also been born in France, the child of American expatriates. "I never knew my grandparents," she said. "They died before I was born. I always think of them as characters out of a Fitzgerald novel. He was an artist, and she was an heiress who adored and supported him. It all sounds very romantic, but I don't think my mother had a happy childhood, because they were totally devoted to each other, and she was always an afterthought to whatever was important to them. I have some of his paintings, including one of my grandmother who was his favorite model. But I'm afraid he wasn't a very good artist, and they aren't worth anything to anyone but family."

"What happened to them?" asked Peter.

"They were drowned sailing on the Mediterranean the year my parents were married."

While she was speaking, she leaned toward him, and her hair fell forward on either side of her face like dark silken curtains. He thought of the experiences she had already had, the places she had been, the ease with which she slipped into a foreign language, and he felt for the first time a slight dissatisfaction with his own life. If it ended tomorrow, he thought, or next month, or next year it wouldn't be enough. It just wouldn't be enough. He felt again the cold fear of what lay ahead, and he trembled in spite of the heat of the ballroom.

At that moment she looked into his eyes, and as if she could read his mind, she said, "Listen, sometimes I know things. I don't know how but sometimes I know things."

Her expression was so intent that it took his breath away. He knew that she was about to tell him something terribly important, something that might change his life, but he had no idea what it was.

"Listen," she said again, "you and I, we have a future, and it will be together. Someday, not yet, but someday we will be the most important people in the world to each other, more important than parents or brothers or sisters. It will happen. Sometimes I know things."

Then as he sat staring into her face, unable to move or speak, she slipped her hand inside his tunic over his heart, and taking his hand she placed it on her rib cage over her own heart. "You see," she said, "I hold your heart in my hand. You hold my heart in yours. That is the way it will be. Don't be afraid. You will come home, and I will be here when you do."

He believed her, and he felt the fear that had gripped him for so long loosen its hold. It was not gone but it could be managed and that was all he asked, and when the orchestra began to play, he led her to the floor to dance.

When the band finally shut down for the last time, they left the hotel, and he took her back to the Kembles' apartment in a cab. In the hall outside the door he put his arms around her and held her. He put his cold cheek against hers and kissed her on the lips. "I'll be seeing you," he said and meant it. "Yes, you will," she said, and kissed him again before she slipped through the door.

Out on the street he decided to walk the twenty blocks back to his parents' apartment. Maria, he thought, Maria, rhymes with—what had she said?—papaya, that was it—a tropical fruit. It made him think of a popular radio jingle, an advertisement for bananas. The tune ran through his head. "Maria Papaya," he sang out loud, and he felt happier and braver than he had in a long time. "Maria Papaya, oh, Maria Papaya".

# Roman Epiphany

In the summer of 1951, Ruth Chapman's husband Charles won an appointment as aide to a friend of his father-in-law's, who was on a special Commission of the State Department to NATO. Charles had been at State for several years, ever since he got back from the South Pacific, and none of his assignments so far had been very interesting. He was therefore quite pleased to have this new job, even though he suspected his father-in-law had played some role in his getting it.

"Oh, Charles," said Ruth, "does this mean we'll be living in Brussels?"

She was young, ten years younger than Charles, and because she had grown up during W.W.II, she had never been to Europe. Charles had been on two grand tours with his family before the war started, and although he was so young then that he remembered very little of those experiences, he liked to refer to them often enough to impress Ruth with his worldliness.

"Of course, dear. That's where NATO has its headquarters. You'll like Brussels. As I remember, it has a fine art museum." In fact he had no memory at all of any museum in Brussels, but he was sure that was a safe enough statement.

"And will we have a house of our own?"

"Well, I believe we will," said Charles, making a mental note to ask about housing the next day at the Department.

In fact they were given a well appointed apartment and a handsome allowance for servants to take care of it. Ruth had not lived so well since her childhood when her parents had had three servants in their Richmond home. This level of comfort did not survive the war in the States, but many Americans recovered it in the shambles and poverty that the war left behind in Europe.

Ruth loved Brussels. She went sight-seeing all over the city and to Bruges and Antwerp as well. ("The Brussels Museum is just as wonderful as you remember it," she told Charles.) She also shopped. All over Europe people were selling their fine possessions for American dollars to rebuild their lives or just to survive. Ruth accumulated treasures almost every day. "Charles, look at this desk (vase, tray, crystal, set of chairs, bed frame…) Isn't it beautiful? And I got it for a song."

The Americans on the Commission frequently entertained delegates from other countries, and there were military parties, as well as parties at all the embassies. At Christmas the King gave a reception at the palace. It was in the palace conservatory, a giant structure filled with huge tropical trees, and the food was the most elaborate Ruth had ever seen. The only thing she didn't like about Belgium was the winter weather, which was miserably cold, damp, and dark.

In January, Charles asked for and received a two weeks leave. Their parents wanted them to come home, but Ruth was anxious to go to some other country in Europe.

"Charles, your next assignment may be some jungle spot in the middle of Africa. We should really see what we can while we're here. Please let's go to Italy. It must be warmer there, and there are so many things to see. I've always dreamed of going to Italy."

He could hardy refuse her, she was so eager. And so in late January they took the train to Milan, where they stayed for two nights and were guided by a gray-faced former art history professor whose oft repeated description of the female statues of Bernini's "too plompah, too heavy" reduced Ruth to schoolgirl giggles.

Then they went on to Pisa, Florence, Amalfi, Capri, Pompeii, and finally to Rome.

"Oh Lord," mourned Ruth, "We'll have to come back over and over. I'm already forgetting what we've seen."

They decided to treat themselves to a special evening on their last night in Rome before a midnight train back to Belgium. The hotel staff had been suggesting they try dinner and dancing at Casa Verdi. "You will like it. All Americans like it. Trust me."

Which, of course was just what Charles didn't do. "They probably get paid for every customer they send there," he said. But then an attractive woman from New York made the same suggestion, and he made a reservation.

When they entered, Ruth saw that Casa Verdi was a kind of Roseland of Rome. There was a large central dancing space and around it many tables, perhaps seventy-five, each with a few flowers in a glass jar and a small red dish with a lighted candle. The orchestra, on an elevated platform at one end of the room, was playing Big Band tunes from the forties. ("Real music, for a change," said Charles.) They were shown to a good table at the edge of the dance floor, and after they ordered, they went out on it to dance.

Charles had taken dancing lessons soon after he joined State. He had, of course, like all little boys at Riverdale Country Day, gone to Mr. Barkley's Dance Classes on Friday afternoons, but he thought for his new career, he should polish his skills. He had certainly improved them, thought Ruth, as they circled the floor in a well-executed fox trot with a number of swirls and reversals. But there was still the same old problem when they danced together. He was a foot taller than she and had never learned to adjust his height to her smallness. He leaned over her, forcing her to arch her back and twist her neck. Their bodies were not in sync. In minutes the muscles in her upper back and shoulders locked into agonizing spasms, and she had to ask to go back to the table. Charles, who had received many compliments on his dancing since his arrival in Belgium, had no idea that that he had anything to do with her problem and found her quick retreat annoying. However, the orchestra took a break just after they sat down, and their food arrived soon after and was far better than he had expected, so he was soon mollified.

Ruth, always an eager observer, saw the two couples first. They were sitting together on the opposite side of the room just across from the Chapmans, and when the music began again, they rose to dance. The women were large and both had hennaed hair and were heavily made up. It was hard to guess their ages, but Ruth thought they must be at least seventy. They were dressed flamboyantly in pre-war fashions, one in a long black dress with beads and sequins, the other in a purple outfit with a multitude of ruffles. They each wore a considerable amount of jewelry, but they were too far away for Ruth to tell whether it was real or not.

The two men with them were no more than thirty, perhaps a good bit younger. Their hair was pomaded, their suits were threadbare and ill-fitting, but worst of all were their shoes, worn and scuffed, the laces broken and knotted. The stitching that held the soles to the shoes of one of the men was completely gone, and the soles were tied to the shoes by pieces of string. Ruth was reminded of a circus clown she had seen when she was a child. His soles had flapped loosely from his shoes, and as a result, he tripped and stumbled and tripped again until he finally fell off a platform into a tub of water, to the huge amusement of the crowd.

But this young man was no clown; his predicament was real. Clearly he was a fine dancer and for moments of time, he was able to lead his partner through a complicated series of steps, but then those damnable flapping soles would throw him off balance and cause him (and his partner) to lose the rhythm of the dance. Finally she gave up and returned to their table. He followed, apologizing, but she was obviously greatly displeased with him. Ruth could see that he was pleading with her about something and that she was shaking her head in refusal. In the end he gave up, and to Ruth's horror, he put his head in his hands and began to cry. No one among the diners and the dancers seemed to notice his pain, no one but Ruth. It occurred to her for the first time that many people here might have observed and experienced so much suffering during the war that they couldn't bear any more.

There was something about this young man's humiliation that tore at her heart. The war, which had been over for such a short time, had barely touched her in America. Belgium had escaped lightly compared to other European countries, and she had seen little there of the kind of destruction that had devastated so many European cities. Instead she had danced and partied away the few months they had been there and ignored the signs of suffering that would have been clear to her if she had only looked. She thought of all the things she had bought and realized that selling them had been an act of desperation on the part of their owners, and she began to weep in pity for them and for the young man and in shame for her own failure to see what was all about her.

Charles was looking at her in dismay.

"What is it?" he said. "What's wrong, Ruth? Are you ill?"

"Please, Charles, help him. Give him some money, anything."

"Ruth, what's wrong with you? You know I can't do that."

"Why not? Look, Charles, look at his shoes. He needs money to buy shoes. It wouldn't take much. Please, Charles, just give him some money."

"Ruth, listen to me. The man's a common gigolo. I can't give him money. I can't barge into another man's life like that. It would be humiliating for both of us."

"Do you think he would care? Isn't he already humiliated?"

He clenched his jaw and looked at her contemptuously. "I think we'd better leave and go back to the hotel to get our bags for the train. You aren't in any state to stay here." He pulled her out of her chair, threw money on the table, and walked her outside, where, then and only then, he helped her on with her coat, while she continued to weep.

"Don't ever embarrass me like that again," he said in the taxi. "Didn't I tell you that Roger Beals from the Embassy was there? Do you want everybody at the Embassy talking about you tomorrow?"

Ruth didn't care whether everyone in Rome talked about her. I deserve to be talked about, she thought, not because I made a scene, but because I was too blind to make one sooner.

At the hotel he left her in the taxi and went inside to arrange for their bags to be brought out. Ruth knew that he was keeping her out of sight until the signs of her weeping had cleared. When he reappeared they went directly to the train station and to their compartment. They did not speak on the drive and only when necessary on the train. In fact they never spoke again about their evening at Casa Verdi.

Ruth stayed in Brussels for six more months. She continued to go to parties with Charles and to do her own share of entertaining. But she spent most of her spare time as a volunteer at La Maison Des Enfants de la Guerre, an orphanage for children who lost their parents in the war. Here she heard from teachers and attendants painful stories of these children and their families. She rarely spoke of them at home for she could see that they only irritated Charles.

In July she left Brussels and went to her parents' house on Long Island. In the fall she wrote Charles that she was not coming back but instead was enrolling in Social Work School at Columbia, and she asked him for a divorce. She was not surprised when he wrote that he had no idea that she was unhappy in their marriage and begged her to reconsider. She wrote:

*Dear Charles, that you had no clue is a clue. It is why I must have this divorce and why you must too. Someday, and I hope not too long from now, we can be friends again. Just remember that we were first loves and nothing can ever change that. Ruth*

Mostly she was able to forget him or at least to think of him only occasionally. As soon as the divorce was final, she returned to Brussells and adopted two children from La Maison des Enfants and took them back to Long Island with her. She got her M.S.W. and found a job with a social agency in New York.

Charles remarried in a few years and had two children. When his father died, Ruth reestablished relations with his mother whom she had always liked. Charles was in New Zealand on assignment at the time, and Ruth thought that Mrs. Chapman was lonely and needed someone to look after her. And so she visited her once or twice a week for many years, for Charles was almost always out of the country. She heard from her about Charles' wife and liked what she heard. She also heard about his children as they grew into adolescence. When Charles was in the States, Mrs. Chapman tactfully let Ruth know, and Ruth was careful not to visit when Charles might be with her. Their only contact for almost thirty years was the sympathy letter she wrote him when his wife died of breast cancer, and his reply.

And so it was a great surprise to her about a year later when Mrs. Chapman invited her to dinner to celebrate her own 89$^{th}$ birthday, and she found that she and Charles were the only two guests.

"I hope you don't mind, my dear," said her mother-in-law (Ruth had long since stopped thinking of her as an ex-mother-in-law), while Charles was in the kitchen. "He's just retired, and I think he's bored and lonely. Actually, he asked me to invite you."

Ruth didn't mind at all. It seemed natural to her that she should be here with him, the man, the only man who had been her husband. He looked the same, or maybe he didn't: same tall slim figure (he'd always worn clothes well), same gray eyes, a little faded perhaps, all that thick dark hair that he was always trying to tame, now totally white and thinned by time to dignified manageability, white eyebrows to match, teeth still straight and even (were they real?), crows' feet at the corners of his eyes, deeper wrinkles in his forehead and cheeks. And his voice, that deep baritone voice that she had loved from the day she met him—that hadn't changed. I believe I married him just to live with that voice, she thought.

And what was he seeing, she wondered. More of me, of course. I must be fifteen pounds heavier than I was when I left him. Hair, blonde—good Lord, I bet that's a shock. Legs still good. Ditto skin. Well, there are some wrinkles, but they're really fine ones. I haven't let myself go like a lot of single women. If I'd known I'd be seeing him, I would have worn something a little dressier, but I guess I'll pass muster.

"I've arranged for us to eat downstairs in the dining room," said Mrs. Chapman. "We'll have drinks there too."

Her expensive apartment building had a restaurant on the ground floor which was used primarily by the residents. This and other amenities made it possible for a number of elderly women like Mrs. Chapman to live there independently.

"But before we go down, Mother," said Charles, "won't you please open your presents?"

Ruth remembered that one of Charles' endearing qualities was his pleasure in buying and giving gifts, and she could see that he had brought several for his mother. The first that she opened held a large cashmere shawl. It had a black background and was covered with bright red poppies.

"Oh, Charles, how beautiful! It's just what I need. I seem to get cold more easily than I used to, and I don't like struggling into sweaters. You remembered how much I love red, and you know how your father always liked to see me wear it. I think I've gotten a little old for red dresses, but this black wrap with the poppies will be perfect. Thank you so much, my dear," and she motioned him to come to her side for a kiss."

The next gift was a box of a very special kind of chocolates that Ruth knew Mrs. Chapman was inordinately fond of and that were difficult to obtain in the U.S.

"Where on earth did you find these, Charlie?" she said. "I haven't had any like this in ages. Oh dear, I think I'm going to be bad and eat one right now. Won't you both join me?"

She popped a chocolate in her mouth and feigned an expression of shame. Charles and Ruth laughed, but refused to join her in this indulgence.

"They're all for you, Mother," laughed Charles, winking at Ruth who was surprised when he handed the last gift to her.

When she opened it, she gave a little gasp of amazement.

"Why, Charles," she exclaimed, "It's *Nos Nuits*, my favorite perfume. I haven't been able to find it in years. I thought it wasn't being made anymore."

He smiled in obvious pleasure at having pleased her.

In the dining room the table conversation was free flowing and animated. Charles and Ruth talked about their children, not a difficult subject as it turned out, for Mrs. Chapman had been informing him about Ruth's at the same time that she had been keeping her up to date on his. He said he could hardly believe she was a grandmother, she was just much too young, and she reminded him that her children were seven and ten when she adopted them. "I got a real head start that way," she said, and asked him about his daughters.

"Jenny's a junior at the University of Michigan. She's in love with a nice young man from Chicago, also a junior, but who knows if this is just one in a series of romances or the real thing. She's still awfully young."

"Not much younger than I was when we married," said Ruth.

"Well, yes," he said. "And I wasn't so young. But I was green, out of my depth in that heady Brussels foreign service society, and scared to death that I was going to disgrace myself and screw up my first overseas assignment. I've often wondered if everything might have been different if we had met when we were older, and I was a little wiser and a little less pompous."

Ruth understood that this was an admission that he had a role in the failure of their marriage. She was so surprised that all she could say was, "We were both young and green, Charles," and then she asked about his older daughter.

"Roberta," he said. "Well, Roberta has finished college and is teaching school in a very rough neighborhood in Boston. I worry about her safety, but she seems to feel she has a mission. She inherited quite a bit of money from her mother, and I told her she doesn't *have* to teach in such a dangerous environment, that there are other places that need teachers. And you know what she said to me? She said, "All that money is just why I *do* have to teach here, Daddy.""

Ruth looked at his face and saw that along with his concern for his daughter, he admired her courage and was proud of her.

"You would like her, Ruth. I wish you two could meet each other."

"Yes, I'd like that too," said Ruth, and meant it.

His mother asked about his new job, "his retirement job," as he called it. He said someone had told him "never just retire, always retire into something," and that was what he was doing. He was going to be a television consultant on the countries along the western border of Russia, which were where his most recent postings had taken him. Both women agreed that it sounded like the perfect job for him. He would be wonderful on television, they said.

About this time another resident of the building arrived for dinner and passed very close to their table. Mrs. Chapman nodded and smiled at her and the man who accompanied her, who Ruth assumed was her son. They were seated at a table for two against the opposite wall.

Ruth looked at the couple more closely. The woman was small and plump with a happy, round face. Her companion was an unusually handsome man. They were leaning into each other across the table, talking, laughing, so pleased to be together.

"Aren't they lovely?" said Mrs. Chapman, with an undisguised twinkle in her eye. "He's a model with one of the big agencies here in the city."

"A model?" said Charles, raising his eyebrows imperceptibly.

Ruth felt her heart catch. Don't let him start in, she thought.

"And he's just gotten a big contract with Brooks Brothers and another to make commercials for the Hyatt Hotels."

"How wonderful," said Ruth. "His mother must be so proud of him."

"Not exactly the career I'd choose for a son of mine," said Charles. "But—to each his own."

"His mother is dead," said Mrs. Chapman, and it was clear by this time that she was enjoying a joke on her guests.

"Then who is that lady with him?" asked Ruth, ever willing to be the straight guy for her hostess.

"That's Louise Greer, "said Mrs. Chapman, "and he's her lover."

Ruth and Charles stared at Mrs. Chapman. Was this a joke? Then they looked again at Mrs. Greer and her companion.

"How old is she?" asked Charles.

"In her mid-eighties, I believe."

"But he can't be over fifty."

"Fifty-two, to be exact." Oh, how she was enjoying their confusion. "They've been lovers for thirty years. She and her husband met Lester at a party long ago. As she tells it, they both thought he was the most beautiful creature they'd ever seen, so they offered to sponsor him if he wanted to go to Hollywood. They hadn't a doubt that he would be a success, but although he had a few bit parts, he couldn't seem to make a real break-through. And so they invited him to come back to New Jersey and live with them. Then soon after he joined them, Mr. Greer died, and she and he have been together for thirty years.

"Isn't she a dear? Everyone here loves her. She's so cheerful and happy. She's clever too: she was editor of an important home furnishings magazine for years before she retired. And he's so sweet to all of us old ladies. Sometimes he sings for us after dinner on Fridays. I hope you'll get to hear him next time you come."

Ruth looked across the table at Charles. His expression was grave and thoughtful. It's so beautiful, Ruth thought. Please, please, don't say anything to spoil it. But he only smiled at her and turned to his mother and asked for the key to her apartment.

"There's something I brought that I forgot to bring down," he said. "Will you excuse me for a moment?"

He was back almost at once with two bottles of champagne. He put one on his mother's table and carried the other across the room to Mrs. Greer's. They could see him introducing himself and shaking hands with her companion, who had sprung to his feet at his approach. When he presented the champagne to Lester, Mrs. Chapman said, "Oh, how nice. He's giving it in honor of Lester's new contracts."

Ruth saw that it must be so. As he returned to them, he watched her face all the way across the room, with a question in his eyes.

What is he asking, wondered Ruth. Is he saying, do you see how I have changed from that pompous young man I was when we married? Is he asking if we can be friends again? Or perhaps he wants us to be more than friends. She had no idea what his question would be, but to her own surprise, she knew that her answer would be yes. And so when he stood before her, she smiled at him and put her hand in his, and he bent to brush it with his lips.

# Mary, Mary

Everyone, including Mary herself, agreed that she could be difficult. She was born a contrarian, and despite her mother's best efforts to modify this aspect of her daughter's personality, and Mary's own desire to be more agreeable, she did not, seemingly could not, change. Her mother used to feel that Mary never got over the "terrible two's." Eventually she gave up temper tantrums and learned to mask, sometimes even to control her fierce determination to have her way, but there was still inside her a little demon that told her "they are wrong and you are right—make them admit it." So say "white" to Mary, and you got back "black," or "up" and she gave you "down." "Mary, Mary, quite contrary," her mother used to say to her sadly, "What am I going to do with you?"

She came by her contentious nature naturally. Her brother was the same, and so was their father and his brother and her grandmother and, if legend could be believed, generations of the Patterson family. Mary had vivid memories from girlhood of her father and her uncle getting together every Sunday afternoon, presumably to watch football or some other spectator sport on television. They would hardly be seated on the couch with their beer and potato chips when the real sport would begin. One would make a provocative remark, the other would respond with indignation, and they were off.

"They ought to get rid of that Wildcat Roberts. He's messing up the whole line. He hasn't made a decent run since the season started, and he can't catch worth a damn."

"What about that twenty-yard catch on the fourth down with Cleveland last week? The Boilers made a touchdown because he got them a first down with that catch."

"Hell, he couldn't have missed that ball with both arms in casts. The team had taken out every Cleveland player on his side of the field. And after he caught it, he stumbled over his own feet and went down when he had a clear field for a touchdown."

"He was in the right place at the right time, and that's half the game, which you would know if you had ever played."

"I suppose a year on the junior varsity in high school qualifies you as a tactical expert?"

"It's more football than you ever played."

At this point the two sisters-in-law would roll their eyes and slip away to the kitchen where they would spend the rest of the afternoon drinking coffee and gossiping and sometimes complaining about their husbands.

"Mules, a family of mules," Mary's mother often said.

"Talking mules," agreed her sister-in-law, "but oh, don't they enjoy themselves!" And she would smile at the sound of the loud voices coming from the den. She found the men more amusing than Mary's mother did, but then she didn't have her mother-in-law living under her roof, arguing day in and day out with Mary's father. The old lady sat in the den with the men on Sundays, knitting and listening to her two sons with a sly smile on her face. She was still capable of besting either of them and often did, but when they were together, she preferred to sit on the sidelines and egg them on with such remarks as "That's where you're wrong, Richard," or "You've missed the point, John." Like a picador among the bulls, she pierced the thick hide of first one and then the other, goading them to charge each other again and again.

During the several hours they spent together, the brothers' arguments would range over a wide variety of subjects, and they were always heated. It might seem to an observer that the two were on very bad terms with each other. On the contrary, they were devoted and thoroughly enjoyed these confrontations. Other brothers might have achieved the same gratification from playing a highly competitive game of one-on-one on a basketball court or smashing tennis balls at each other across a net. At the end of the day they went out to Mary's uncle's car to say their good-bys with their arms draped over each other's shoulders, laughing loudly, faces flushed, adrenaline still pumping. For them it had been an extremely satisfying afternoon of verbal wrestling with many points awarded, and no winners or losers.

When she was a child, Mary found these confrontations frightening and chose to stay close to the women in the kitchen. But by the time she was a teenager, she was engaged in the same kind of exhilarating arguments with her own brother. She and Teddy could go on for hours on the most inconsequential subjects. Later when they were both in college, they took opposite sides on more weighty topics of politics and social philosophy. Mary was convinced that Teddy had adopted a very conservative stance simply because she was strongly inclined toward liberalism. She enjoyed these heated discussions, although sometimes when her father weighed in on Teddy's side, she felt overwhelmed by their masculinity, their loud voices and powerful assertiveness. She realized that when she shouted or demanded her turn to be heard that she simply came across as shrill, and she hated the way that tears would sometimes spring to her eyes when she felt they were browbeating her.

"Mary," said her mother, "if you talk to other men the way you do to Teddy and your father, you're never going to get married." Mary noticed that her mother was spending more and more time away from the house playing bridge with her friends.

"I'll find a man who can stand up to me without yelling like Teddy and Daddy do," said Mary.

"Good luck," said her mother.

What Mary had in mind was a man who, however strongly he disagreed with her, would debate the issues civilly. She did not expect or want a husband whose opinions were a carbon copy of her own, or worse, were lightly formed and weakly held. Such a marriage, she thought, would be bland, lacking in spice. And she liked the vigorous argument of differences, not just for the purposes of resolving them, but also because she needed verbal sparring to feel alive in the way an athlete needs to exercise. But sparring, she said to herself, is different from the slug-it-out boxing matches that the most recent arguments with Teddy and her father had become. When Mary tried to explain to her mother that she would see that arguments in her marriage would be fencing matches rather then duels to the death, her mother just shook her head sadly and raised her eyebrows.

When she went off to college, Mary found that her mother was mostly right. She was a pretty girl, and there were men who found her feistiness interesting, even attractive at first, but after a few dates, they turned away from her to the girls who smiled and agreed with them. The only ones who continued to want to see her were as obstreperous as Teddy and her father. They seemed to take some kind of malevolent pleasure in overriding with loud voices whatever she tried to say or in ridiculing her opinions. She could almost give as good as she got, but it wasn't fun.

Then one night a date, with whom she was having a spirited conversation on the dance floor, backed off, looked down at her and said, "You never give up, do you? Why don't you just join the debating team and be done with it?" And he walked off the floor and never came back. She was humiliated, but it occurred to her that he might have given her good advice, which she decided to take.

And for a while it seemed to work. By the end of her junior year she had won more points than anyone in her college league, and as a senior, she came in third in a nationwide collegiate contest.

Her success was gratifying to her, but the boys were still not lining up to date her, and much as she wished they were, she couldn't seem to change who she was. When someone was brave enough to ask her out, she bit her lips trying to control her tongue. But almost inevitably she lost the battle and blurted out a direct contradiction of some long held conviction that blew her date away. That she had learned to say, "I believe you are mistaken on that point" instead of "You're just plain dead wrong," was not enough to save the day.

It was no better at home. Using her debating skills and the principles of logic she had studied at college, she only managed to infuriate her father and brother. "Mary, what's the point of taking them on when you only make them mad at you?" said her mother. Mary began to wonder if she should take up bridge with her mother to escape from the men in the house, but when she made that suggestion, mostly in jest, her mother looked at her long and hard. "I presume you're joking," she said. "You and I have had a pretty good mother-daughter relationship up to now. Let's keep it that way."

When she finished college, she found a job in the advertising department of an appliance company. It was a large factory industry with its headquarters in the small town near Chicago where her family lived. Mary liked her work and was good at it. She wrote clever copy and made amusing amateurish sketches to show the department's artists how she wanted her text illustrated. It wasn't long before she was winning awards from the Chicago Advertising Council and getting job offers from advertising firms in the city. She chose to stay where she was because she disliked the idea of an hour commute into Chicago. Also she liked the job she had, and as she advanced in the department, she could see a successful career for herself right there. It's a good thing I can do something well, she thought. I don't seem to be successful at attracting men, but at least I can earn a living. Mother is probably right; it doesn't look as though I'll ever be married.

She had been with Anderson Industries for several years, when she met Hank Fellows. She had heard his name, of course. He was a salesman from a firm in Chicago that supplied many of the parts for Anderson products, and he was said to be the absolute best in his profession, but he had no reason to call on the advertising department and Mary had had no contact with him. But on the day they met, she was having an earlier than usual lunch in the company cafeteria instead of at her desk, and he was there roaming the room, talking to Anderson employees, just before his afternoon appointment with production officers of the company.

Mary was in the food line when she heard the stranger in front of her say to a man ahead of him, "How is that new package system working out for you people, Pete?"

"It's just great, Hank. I figure our team saves ten man-hours a day not having to get those switches out of that bubble wrap and tape stuff."

"Glad to hear it. Any new problems we can work together on?"

"Can't think of anything just now. I heard someone on the line complaining that it's hard to insert those new fuses into the panel box, but I don't know—maybe he's just got big hands. Anyway, he's at that table over there, guy in the red shirt, if you want to ask him yourself."

"Thanks, Pete. Will do."

But as he continued down the cafeteria line to get his lunch, he turned back to talk to whoever was behind him, and when that turned out to be Mary, he never made it to the man in the red shirt. In fact, he almost missed his sales meeting.

"Hello," he said, "I'm Hank Fellows from the Berkwell Company. We make a lot of the parts for your larger appliances, and I always like to ask the people who put the machines together how we're doing. If you know any way we can improve our product, I'd sure like to hear it."

It was his usual approach. Most workers welcomed the opportunity to sound off on their problems and complaints to Hank. He had a reputation for finding solutions to problems and sharing credit with the workers who helped him. But Mary was trying to assemble the condiments to go with her hamburger, and she hardly gave him a glance.

"Sorry. I don't think I can help you," she said. "I work in the advertising department, so I don't have any first hand knowledge of your products." Then she looked at him and wished she had not dismissed him so cavalierly, for there was something immensely appealing to her about his face. It's not his features, she said to herself, or even the way they come together, although they're pleasing enough. It's something in his expression, a brightness, an openness. He looks kind. He looks—content. If I could just keep looking and looking at that face...At the same moment he was saying, "Won't you please eat with me anyway? I'd like to learn more about the advertising department."

And then they were both laughing, and they continued to laugh all through lunch, and to talk about anything but his products and her advertising department. When Hank realized he was about to be late for his meeting, he asked her to have dinner with him later. "I don't usually hang around after my calls, but you are the best incentive to linger I can imagine," he said, and Mary had no problem accepting his invitation.

Back in her office she tried to finish a piece of copy she was working on, but knowing that Hank was in another office down the hall was so distracting that at three o'clock she gave up and left early to get her hair done. She also bought a new lipstick and a bottle of very expensive perfume. She observed herself doing these things as if she were someone else. You must be losing your mind, she said. You know you always blow it sooner or later, so why set yourself up to do it again, especially with this guy? The more special they are, the more it hurts when they walk away, and, admit it, this Hank Fellows is special. When have you ever walked out on the job to make yourself pretty for a date? You'll have to stay up all night getting that copy ready for tomorrow morning's meeting.

I don't care, she told herself. I think this may be the most important night of my life, and I don't care if I don't sleep tonight or any night the rest of this week, if I can just not screw up this date.

At home she told her mother she wouldn't be home for dinner and went upstairs to dress. When she came down in her best outfit, her mother looked her over. She noted the careful make-up and the scent of the new perfume and something else, some barely suppressed excitement that Mary was struggling to contain.

"Important company party?" she asked, already sure that it was not.

"Nope, a date with a visiting salesman."

"If he inspires you to wear those pumps, he must be special. I know they hurt your feet. Why don't you put on something more comfortable?"

"Mom, I bought them to go with this dress, and they look great with it. What's a little pain for the sake of beauty? Just call me the little mermaid." And she was out the door.

Her mother listened until she heard Mary's car start. "Oh, my dear, my dear," she said out loud. "I hope you can keep that inner lion of yours on a tight leash tonight. I have a feeling this time it really matters."

She need not have worried. Hank gave Mary no opportunity to disagree with him. He asked her to order for him because she was familiar with the restaurant and he was not. He told her she had chosen his favorites and that they were all delicious. He told her she was beautiful and smart and interesting and funny. He took her out to the dance floor and praised her footwork. And he told her about his work. His philosophy as a salesman, he said, was that he was there to help his customers by saving them time or money. Salesmen who were only interested in pushing their products and increasing their commissions would never be more than run-of-the-mill, he told her.

How could she disagree with anything he said? If he thought she was beautiful and interesting, then she must be. Dancing with him was a sensation so delicious, how could she not float in perfect lockstep, her temple pressed against his cheek? And surely he must be the best salesman in the world, for how could anyone resist his charm? She found him in every way irresistible.

At the end of dinner he asked if she would meet him again, "same time, same place," on his way back to Chicago on Friday night. When he said good night at her car, he didn't try to kiss her, but gave her a quick hug that left her breathless. What does that hug mean, she wondered, as she drove home? Was it just an ordinary friendly hug or was it something more? If it was something more, then why didn't he kiss me? Oh, Lord, I can't bear it if he just wants to be friends. How can I wait until Friday to see him again?

Friday night was much like Monday, except that this time at the car he did kiss her, and it was as wonderful as she had imagined. Don't let this moment end, she prayed, but at last it did and she had to drive home. "Monday night?" he said as they parted. Two down and how many to go, she thought.

It was on their third date that she blew it. They had discovered their mutual interest in vintage films, and were discussing their favorite comedians from movies they had seen as children. "I really loved the Marx brothers," said Mary. "They were the *crème de la crème*."

"Yes," said Hank, "they were funny all right, but I think the Three Stooges were even funnier."

"How can you say that?" cried Mary before she could stop herself. "Juvenile slapstick, that's all they could ever did. Their idea of subtlety was a pie in the face. Only a kid could compare them with the Marx Brothers."

She caught herself, pressed her fingers to her mouth, horrified by what she had said. How could she have spoken to him like that? What would he think of her? That hateful uncontrollable demon inside her had lashed out at the only person she had ever wanted to spend the rest of her life with. What would he do? Strike out at her in a similar tone or freeze into silence? Make polite conversation through the rest of their meal together, and then walk away when he took her to her car and never see her again?

She stared at him but could not read his expression. His brow was knit, his eyes startled, his mouth compressed. When, after an hour long thirty seconds he finally spoke, his tone was mild.

"Mary," he said thoughtfully, "I think you're right. I haven't seen them since I was a child, and I'm still looking at them with my little boy eyes. I thought all that silly slapstick stuff was hilarious when I was a kid, but I probably wouldn't as an adult. How about we get a Marx Brothers video and watch it together next week when I'm here."

And that was all. So that's how it is with you, she thought. You won't let me fight with you; no arguments allowed. She found the idea curiously reassuring. Is it possible that inside this woman warrior there is an undiscovered peacenik after all, she wondered? She let out the breath she had been holding for what seemed like hours, and smiled at him. When he returned her smile, she felt she had been given a benediction.

That was the night that she tried to tell him about her little demon. "He multiplies in my family tree," she said. "All of the Pattersons have one, it seems. Sometimes he gets out of hand." That was as far as she was ready to go, and she was glad when he brushed aside her confession as though it were of no significance.

Another test lay ahead—her family. How would they react to him, and, more important, how would he deal with their pit bull approach to human relations? The question was answered when he came for a Sunday afternoon visit the following weekend. Mary's grandmother had died while Mary was in college, but her uncle and his wife were still part of family get-togethers, and Teddy was there as well. When Hank arrived, all the men were in the den settling down to watch a Sunday afternoon pro game, and they were already arguing over the political interview shows they had just seen.

"Come in, come in," said Mary's father. "This is my brother Richard and my son Teddy. Come right in and help settle this little disagreement we've been having. Is that expression on George Bush's face a smirk or a smile? I say it's a smile. Nice guy—smiles a lot. Nothing wrong with that. Richard and Teddy say it's a smirk. They don't like him, so it's a smirk. Just look at this picture in today's paper. If that isn't a perfectly fine smile, I never saw one. What do you say, Hank?"

Hank studied the picture for a long time with fierce concentration while the other three men and Mary waited for him to express his opinion. Mary knew it was a trap, that whatever he said, those who disagreed would come roaring into the fray in opposition, but by now she had confidence in his ability to fend for himself.

"I think," he finally said, "that this is a man who has a smile—a slightly flawed smile that sometimes looks as if it might be a smirk. In fact, I believe it is a both a smiley smirk and a smirky smile."

For a moment the other three men stared at him in silence. Was he mocking them? But then he smiled his own broad smile, laughed his loud contagious laugh, and clapped them each on the shoulder in turn, and soon they were all laughing with him and urging him to join them and watch the game.

"But I haven't met Mary's mother," he said. And so Mary took his hand and led him back to the kitchen where her mother and her Aunt Lucile were finishing the dishes. Hank offered to help, but they made him sit down and poured him a cup of coffee and cut him a piece of cake. When they were done with the dishes, they sat down with him, and he told them about how he had met Mary in the cafeteria and about their first date that evening. He complimented Lucile on the cake she had baked and asked for a second piece, and he told Mary's mother that it was easy to see where Mary got her good looks. By the time her dad came in the kitchen to tell him the game was starting, Mary was red with embarrassment and pleasure. She stayed behind just long enough for her mother to say to her, "Mary, I think you've got yourself a keeper."

And she did. They were married a few weeks later, and she moved into his apartment in Chicago and took one of the high powered advertising jobs she had been offered in the city. Mary had never been so happy in her life. The only downside was the frequent out-of-town sales trips that Hank had to make, but these only fueled her pleasure in his company when he returned. Was this overwhelming joy in his presence the balm that had soothed her contrarian nature, she wondered, as months passed without incident?

The first sign that her demon was not dead but merely asleep came at the Berkwell Christmas party. Mary wore a new red Christmas dress and the diamond earrings that Hank had given her for a wedding gift, and he presented her to his fellow employees as if she were a gold Olympic medal he'd just won. Finally he led her over to a small group of five or six men, but before he could introduce her, she heard one of them say, "Well, of course they can sell consumer products—household items, clothes, that sort of thing. What I'm telling you is that women don't belong on the sales force of industrial companies like Berkwell. They just can't talk the talk when it comes to pitching to production engineers or research and development managers."

"Surely you don't mean that," said Mary.

"As a matter of fact I do," replied the man who had spoken. Something about the way he reared back to look at her and the severity of his expression should have warned her that this was a man who was not accustomed to being challenged, but Mary heard the old familiar cry of battle and she plunged ahead undaunted.

"Then I think you need to rethink your opinion," she said. "Many women today have degrees in engineering and are expert researchers. They can talk intelligently with anyone in the field, and they tend to have better human relations skills and sharper intuition than most men, which should make them good salespeople of any product." She was about to go on, but she could feel Hank behind her tugging at her dress and was momentarily distracted. Then she noticed the apprehensive expressions on the faces of the other men in the group. They were watching the man to whom she was speaking, and when he finally gave Mary a wry smile and nodded at her, there was a visible relaxation of tension.

"Point well taken. You're Hank's wife, aren't you?" he said. "I've heard about you. Rising star at the Buell Agency. Maybe we should move our account to your people. Keep the business in the family, so to speak. Something to think about anyway. Wife's a star, Hank. Pretty *and* smart. My wife was pretty and smart too. Kind of woman I like."

And before anyone could respond, he moved away with his entourage at his heels.

"Gosh, Mary, that's Henry Anderson. He owns the company. You never know how he'll react to anything, but obviously he liked you. I don't mind telling you I was really scared when you lit into him. I thought he might be angry, and I would have to try to defend you, and I would certainly do that, but it wouldn't be easy to take on my boss."

Mary was contrite. "Oh, Hank, I'm so sorry. I do try, but sometimes things just pop out. I don't know why you're not furious at me."

"I could never be mad at you, Mary. I promise you that little demon of yours isn't ever going to come between us."

Mary did try, and it was only occasionally that she lost control and lit into someone. I think I've almost got it licked, she said to herself, after several months without what she referred to as "one of my episodes." It's just a matter of saying "You have an interesting take on that" or "I never thought of it from that perspective" instead of wading in with both fists up. But when she was honest with herself, she admitted that she missed the rush of energy that came with a real knock-down, drag-out argument.

Several months after the Christmas party, Hank asked her if she would help him entertain a customer. "He's not just any customer, Mary. He's my biggest customer. I sell him over a million dollars worth of parts every year. He lives in Iowa, and every now and then he comes to Chicago, and I take him out to some real posh place for dinner. Usually he comes alone, but this time he's bringing his wife. I haven't met her, but if she's like him, she's a real small town type. 'Prudish,' I guess, is the best word to describe him. Religious fundamentalist, I think, and he wouldn't put up with her being any different. It won't be a fun evening, but it would help if you were there."

"Sounds like a swell party—I can't wait," said Mary. "Sure, I'll come. After all, I did pledge 'for better, for worse.'"

"And, Mary, remember this fellow is my best customer, and he has no sense of humor like Henry Anderson. In fact, he riles easily, so try not to cross him."

It was the first time he had ever referred to what she had come to think of as her problem, and she realized that this evening with the Parsons was even more crucial to him than she had thought. She vowed to herself that no matter how difficult the Parsons were, she would not take issue with them.

But when she and Hank met with them, it was apparent that Hank had reason to warn her. They were as difficult and unattractive a couple as Mary had ever met. Mary had deliberately dressed down for the evening, and she saw at once that she had done the right thing, for Mrs. Parsons, who was wearing all black, looked as if she had dressed in mourning to do the laundry. She was a small woman with frizzed gray hair, tightly pursed lips, and steel rimmed bifocals. Her husband was almost as small as she was with the same pursed lips and frizzy hair. (Do they give each other home permanents, wondered Mary?)

Introductions were quickly made, and the maitre d' showed them to their table. A waiter came to take their drink order, and as Mrs. Parsons was hesitating, Mary spoke up first and asked for a scotch and soda.

"I'm surprised you allow your wife to drink, Hank," said Mr. Parsons. "I don't oppose it on religious grounds, although there are some who do. After all, our Lord himself turned water into wine. However, it can result in very unseemly behavior, especially in young women. In fact, I remember an occasion when a young woman about your wife's age drank to excess at one of our company picnics and…" He was off on a long and sordid anecdote while the waiter shifted from one foot to the other and finally disappeared.

Mary swallowed the words that were rising in her throat. She could feel that Hank was watching her anxiously. "You're quite right, Mr. Parsons. I know alcohol has its dangers, and the truth is, I seldom drink. I just got carried away with the pleasure of meeting you and Mrs. Parsons and felt that a celebration was in order. But plain tonic water will be fine."

To her left she heard Hank let out a long breath. You really are worried about me, she thought, but I showed you that time. Then the irony of the situation struck her. Hank and I are in the best steakhouse in Chicago with what must be the most officious man in the world, and we're not even allowed to anesthetize ourselves with a scotch and soda. The situation struck her as funny, and she had to choke back an impulse to laugh out loud.

After two tonics and a half hour of trying to make conversation with Mrs. Parsons while Hank and Mr. Parsons discussed mutual business interests, she had lost her sense of humor. Easy for the men, she grumbled to herself as they went on about gauges and pipes and meters. She made one last attempt to engage Mrs. Parsons, who had made clear her lack of interest in all the cultural aspects of Mary's favorite city.

"So what is it that brings you to Chicago, Mrs. Parsons? Do you have special friends here?" she asked.

"Oh, no, I don't know anyone here. Stanley has a great many friends in the city," (I bet, thought Mary.) "Business friends, that is. He's busy with them most of the day. I rarely come with him. This time I had to because of Bradley. We needed to put him in the hospital, and I have to sit with him there—there's a terrible shortage of nurses, you know, and so I have to be there to rub his back and comfort him. He's such a big baby. He has to have a very serious operation tomorrow, a heart transplant, in fact. We haven't told him yet." And

Mary watched in horror as tears began to stream down Mrs. Parson's face.

"I'm so sorry," she said. "I shouldn't have said whatever I did that made you think of him."

"He doesn't have much of a chance," said Mrs. Parson. "He's almost eleven, not a good age for a transplant. I just don't know what I'll do if anything happens to him. The doctors haven't given us much encouragement. It's clear to me they don't want to do it at all, but when this heart became available, Amos gave the hospital a great deal of money, and they agreed to use it for Bradley."

"I didn't think they let you do that, buy your way to the top of the list. It doesn't seem ethical," said Mary.

"He sleeps in her bed," said Mr. Parsons, as though that explained everything. "We won't dwell on him anymore now, Irma. It only makes you sad to talk about him."

Mrs. Parsons obediently dried her eyes and never spoke again. Fortunately their steaks arrived, and they were diverted from the sad saga of Bradley, although Mary continued to wonder about him silently. Was he their grandchild? Surely they were too old, in their sixties, she guessed, to have a son who was eleven. But what was this about him sleeping in his grandmother's bed, and where were his parents?

To divert the conversation from Bradley, Mary turned to Mr. Parsons and asked him about his children. This was usually a safe ploy with businessmen and women, but in this case, it backfired.

"We have two children," he replied, "but they live in San Francisco, and we have no contact with them. They have chosen a lifestyle that is unacceptable to us, that is the opposite of everything we believe in. There is no disappointment greater than children who reject the path you have chosen for them, as I hope that you and Hank will never have to discover for yourselves. Bradley has taken their place in our hearts. Dogs, at least, are loyal to those who care for them."

Mary could hardly believe what she was hearing. Bradley, a dog! In the hospital for a heart transplant! Their own children disowned because they were not following "the path their parents had chosen for them." She started to speak, but Hank, who was just signing the check for their dinner, interrupted and changed the subject.

"Tell me, Stanley, how do people in Iowa feel about the President and his policies?"

"I cannot speak for all Iowans, Hank, but for myself, I am hopeful. There are three issues I believe are primary: health care, the welfare system, and labor policy."

"Oh, yes, I agree," said Mary, surprised that he should share these concerns so dear to her heart.

"What you probably don't see is the connection between these issues," said Mr. Parsons. "Few people understand that each profoundly affects the other."

"Oh, but I do understand," said Mary. "There are companies that won't pay for health benefits for their workers and fight the unions all the way. That's why there are so many people without insurance, and often they go on welfare just to get medical care, especially if they have children with health problems. Poor things, what else can they do?"

He looked at her as if she had lost her mind. She realized too late that she had misinterpreted his earlier statement. For a moment she thought he was going to tear into her, but then with great effort he composed himself. When he spoke, his tone was so condescending that it was clear that he had decided that her opinion was scarcely worth refuting.

"You are young, my dear," he said, "and can scarcely be expected to grasp the complicated interrelationships involved here. When labor unions demand more and more wages and benefits, companies like mine and your husband's are forced to lay off many workers. Then, of course, those people lose their medical coverage, which, I might add, gets more expensive every year. Often they end up on welfare because they will not accept other work. You, I know, hold a responsible position and therefore understand the importance of diligent work, but this is not the case with most common laborers. They are lazy and have no interest in working harder to improve their productivity. And yet they think it unfair that they don't have the same benefits as responsible people such as you and I who work hard to earn them."

Why, you pompous little ass, thought Mary, and felt the fiery breath of her demon rising in her throat. "I suppose you think it's fair that rich people can buy hearts for dogs while the children of poor people are dying for lack of one," she said.

There was a little gasp from Mrs. Parson, followed by a moment of complete silence at the table. Mary could not bear to look at Hank. Finally, Mr. Parsons stood up and his wife rose as he did.

"Thank you for a fine dinner," he said to Hank. "Perhaps I'll see you at the Convention Hall tomorrow." He took his wife's arm and led her to the coatroom without a word to Mary. Soon they were visible on the street through the plate glass window of the restaurant, and Mary watched Mr. Parsons hale a taxi and drive away.

At the same time she felt Hank take her arm. He was propelling her toward the cloakroom where he retrieved her coat and held it for her to slip into. She was so embarrassed and ashamed of her behavior that she could hardly bear to look at him. I promised him, she thought, I promised him to control myself, and instead I was horrid.

Outside he swung her around to face him. The icy wind stung her eyes, and she saw his face through a blur of tears. So this is what he is like when he finally loses his temper, she thought. His jaw was clenched, and his complexion was an angry red. His eyes were narrowed and his mouth unnaturally compressed. Through his heavy overcoat she could feel his body shaking as he tried to control his emotions. She waited for him to lash out at her. Whatever he says, I deserve it, she told herself.

But when he finally opened his mouth, it was to release a great torrent of laughter. His hot breath turned to a cloud of steam in the cold night air and swirled around their faces so that she could hardly see him. For a moment she doubted what she heard, but then she saw it was true, he was laughing, laughing so hard that he couldn't speak, but could only throw his arms around her in a giant bear hug.

"Oh, Mary, Mary," he gasped finally when he could get his breath. "I'm so sorry. I knew he was awful, but I didn't realize how awful. I could see you were struggling to contain yourself, and you did for longer than I thought possible. Then when you finally let loose, you were splendid. I bet he hasn't been crossed like that since his children moved out."

Mary began to cry. "But he's your customer, your best customer, Hank. Now he probably won't even see you the next time you go to Ames."

"Yes, he will. He probably feels sorry for me because I can't control my wife like he does his. As if I would want to when you are so perfect just as you are. Good God, a heart transplant for a dog!" And Hank began to laugh again until there were tears rolling down his face.

The tightness in Mary's chest gave way as he spoke. A suffocating weight dissolved and rose upward into the dark, icy air. Exorcism by unqualified love, she thought. She took a deep breath, and suddenly she was laughing too. Hank seized her arm, and, clutching each other, they went together, laughing, laughing, into the winter night.

# The Birthday Party

The silver, the silver! It is piled on the kitchen table, and some of it is very tarnished. Where *is* Paul? thinks Hope Waring. Late again, as usual, but over an hour late? And he hasn't even called her. Perhaps he has forgotten that he was supposed to come to her today. She has tried his beeper, but he hasn't responded, and she has no other way to get in touch with him. Surely he knows that she is counting on him to help her get ready for her party tonight. It's a small party to be sure, only her three children and their spouses, but it's such an important celebration, Sam's seventy-fifth birthday and his retirement from the University. She wants it to be perfect. She wants the house to look its best, all the silver and brass gleaming, the just cleaned slipcovers and draperies back in place, the beautiful portrait of Sam, given by the University as a farewell gift, hung over the mantle in the library. She wants this to be a family occasion that none of them will ever forget. She could clean the silver herself if she had time, but she doesn't. Besides, no one polishes metals as well as Paul does, and she needs him for the other chores as well. Where on earth is he?

The phone rings, and she runs to the kitchen to answer it. Oh, let it be Paul, she prays. And it is.

"Paul, thank heavens. I was getting worried that you had the date wrong. I'm so glad you've called."

"I'm sorry, Miz Waring. I had car trouble, but it's getting fixed. I'll be done here by late morning, and then I'll come right over."

Not until almost lunchtime and so much to be done. But she will have to take what she can get. She had planned to shop for flowers in the afternoon, but now she supposes she had better go for them now before Paul comes.

Upstairs Annie is running the vacuum. There is no point in trying to call up to her over the noise, so Hope runs up the stairs and into her bedroom. Annie looks tired. She is heavy and has diabetes, and Hope worries about her.

"Are you feeling all right, Annie?" she asks. "Did you remember to take your medication this morning?"

Hope has reason to worry. Annie fails to take her pills from time to time, and she also sometimes disregards the strict diet she is supposed to follow. As a result, she has on several occasions fallen into a diabetic coma, and Hope has had to call 911 for help. Annie has worked for her for over twenty years, and Hope is fond of her and has at times confided personal problems to her that she has mentioned to no one else. Annie was the only one she told when her pap smear came back positive a year ago. She had not wanted her family to know while she was sweating out the results of a retest that happily was negative. Years earlier she wept in the kitchen with Annie when Hope's only daughter Kathy broke her engagement to a man Hope thought was perfect for her. Annie brought her cups of tea and told her that Kathy had always known what she wanted and how to get it and that Hope shouldn't worry about her, she would do just fine.

"Yes, ma'm, Miz Waring, I took my medicine. I'm tired because I didn't get too much sleep last night. Little Joshie got a coughing cold."

"Oh, Annie, I'm sorry about little Joshie, but you know Doctor Pratt has told you that you have to get your rest. You just can't stay up till all hours and expect not to feel tired the next day. You have to take better care of yourself than that," scolds Hope.

Annie looks at her as if she's about to speak, then sighs, drops her eyes to her feet, and mumbles, "Yes'm."

"Paul called, says he has car trouble and will be here about lunch time. I'm going out now for flowers, should be back in an hour. I pulled out all the silver for tonight and put it on the kitchen table, so he can start with that if he gets here before I get back."

Annie says "yes'm" again and turns the vacuum back on.

It takes stops at three different florists before Hope is satisfied. She is good with flowers, rarely uses arrangements that have been done by florists. She buys lavishly, adds up in her head what she has spent as she leaves the final store, takes a deep breath. That much?! She has probably never spent so much on flowers since Katie's wedding, but she doesn't care. This is an occasion.

When she gets home, she trails the heady fragrance of her purchases into the kitchen where she finds Paul and Annie sitting and drinking coffee. She is glad to see that Paul has arrived, but for a single moment she thinks: why are they sitting when there is so much to do? She is ashamed of the thought as soon as she has it. Annie has been on her feet all morning, and Paul has no doubt had a dreary experience with his car. Paul rises to his feet and shakes her hand. He is Haitian, a proud and independent man. He works as a handyman, and because he can do almost anything around the house, and most of the husbands in this university town can do almost nothing, he is in great demand. Hope has had him lined up for this day for several weeks.

"That's too bad about your car, Paul," she says. "You haven't had it very long. It shouldn't be giving you trouble so soon."

"It isn't my car, Miz Waring, it's my daughter's, an old piece of junk nobody ought to be driving, but it's all she can afford. She couldn't start it this morning, and the folks where she works told her she'd get fired if she was late again. So I had to drive her there and drop off her two kids at the daycare, then go back home and get somebody to help me push her car to the garage down the street. I told them to call me here to tell me the bad news. Never is any good news about that car. Hope that's all right with you."

"Of course, Paul, that'll be fine. Your daughter has a good job now, doesn't she?"

"Yes, she does. Bookkeeping for Loslo's at the mall. But it doesn't pay much. I try to help her whatever way I can. She doesn't get any child support from that no-good."

He gets up from the table, rinses his coffee cup in the sink, gets out the silver polish, and goes to work. Annie begins to make a cake for the party tomorrow. She usually comes only to clean, but for special occasions she will cook and serve dinner. And this is a most special occasion, thinks Hope. All of her children live elsewhere, two in Manhattan and one in Philadelphia, not really far away, but not close enough to Princeton to drop by. She hardly ever sees all three of them at once anymore. They have important careers and lead such busy lives, they need a special invitation, an event, to come to see her and Sam. An ordinary birthday is not enough. But a seventy-fifth birthday *and* a retirement is bringing them all.

She removes the flowers from the green waxed tissue in which they have been wrapped, and brings two pails from a closet and fills them with water. Trimming stems and stripping leaves, she carefully places the flowers in the pails. Their heavy, exotic scent suffuses the kitchen, and even in the plastic pails, they are so beautiful, so extraordinarily beautiful, thinks Hope. She puts her arms around the pails and leans over them to breathe in the fragrance. She has a summer garden, but these hothouse flowers from around the world are so perfect—impossible to imagine so much loveliness, and yet here it is in her own kitchen.

"You sure do love flowers, don't you, Miz Waring?" says Annie. She is working at the island in the center of the kitchen, measuring out flour. "I can tell how important a party is by how many bowls of flowers you have in the house, and this party must be even more important than the one for the Dean last spring, even though you only having eight this time and they all family. Why are you making such a big fuss over them kids?"

Hope laughs. Annie knows exactly how important this party is to her and why it is. Annie likes to tease her. This kind of banter is part of their relationship.

"Because they're such special kids, Annie," she says. "You ought to know that. And we're celebrating some special events in their lives this year as well as in Mr. Waring's. Tom made partner in his law firm, and he and Mary had baby Tommy. Richie says he's had a great year at the brokerage, and he tells me this year is going to be just as good. And Kathy sold more houses than anyone else in her office and won the Real Estate Woman of the Year award in Philadelphia. We're so proud of them. They've all worked so hard and been so successful. Well, you know them, you know how great they are."

"Yes, ma'm, I do," Annie answers.

She doesn't say anything else. Hope tries to sneak a look at her without Annie seeing. She does look tired. Hope wonders again if she has skipped her medicine, but decides not to ask.

She goes out in the yard to cut some greenery for her arrangements, boxwood and juniper and whatever else she can find. Even though it is November, there are still some leaves and branches that she can probably use. The air is nippy, and she returns through the sunroom where she can leave her plant material until she is ready to arrange it. She feels hungry and realizes she hasn't eaten since breakfast, and so she starts back to the kitchen. From just outside the door she hears Annie and Paul talking together. She hesitates a minute, and then something in their voices catches her attention, makes her stand quietly. I can't believe I am doing this, she thinks, eavesdropping on Annie and Paul. It's shameful. But she continues to stand and listen.

"Tara's a good girl at heart. I know that. When her Momma was sick, she stayed by her side, nursing her day and night. But that was two whole years of her high school time, and she missed more days than she went. When Becky died, she was so behind in her schooling, she didn't think she could ever catch up. She was a good student too, before she stayed home so much. When she went back she was so mad and so sad about losing her Momma and so ashamed of being behind, she was just ripe fruit on the vine for that lowlife when he came along. I tried my best to tell her what kind of trash he was, but might as well talk to the deaf. He stayed around just long enough to give her two babies, and now he's off some place, probably making more babies to walk away from. I help her out some, they live with me, and she's tried real hard to make up for all that school she missed. She got a GED, and she took a bookkeeping course and got a half-way decent job, but her littlest has asthma and she worries about her all the time, and, to tell the truth, Annie, sometimes she drinks too much. I don't know, I just don't know."

"Well, at least you got your child with you. You know where Joshua in now, don't you? He's back in jail. Just can't keep off that stuff. It's probably better for him he's in jail, but folks tell me he can even get drugs there. That's why I won't send him no money no matter how hard he begs me. He ain't getting nothing from me for that. He was a good boy till those gang kids came along and ruined him. If his Daddy hadn't died when Josh was only six, he wouldn't be in jail cause his Daddy wouldn't never have stood for him messing up his life like he has. Only consolation I've got is that sweet girl friend of his and their little boy. She's so good to me, that Rosie, better than Joshua's been. She cooks dinner for all of us every night before I get home. I love her like she's my own child. She's trying to get a job, something part time, because she has little Joshie to look after. I tell her, 'Don't worry about getting work. We don't need no more money as long as I can do my cleaning work. You're keeping our place clean and doing the cooking and marketing and taking care of little Joshie, that's plenty. We'll make out fine.' The truth is I'm afraid she'll give money to Joshua if she has any extra. He's been getting whatever he wanted from her as long as she's known him. I love that boy of mine—you know how it is with your own, but I don't see why she got any reason to love him so much."

Standing in the butler's pantry next to the door, Hope can hear that Annie is crying softly.

"Ain't your fault Josh went wrong, Annie," says Paul. "It's just real hard to bring up kids these days. I got hopes for Tara and her kids, but I don't know if my hopes is worth a nickel."

For Hope, still standing outside the kitchen door, these revelations, unintended for her ears are a crack in her small world. She has been aware for a long time that Annie has family problems, but Annie, in spite of their long relationship, has never confided any details to her. All confidences have been one way, from Hope to Annie. And Paul, Paul has a daughter and grandchildren! He has worked at her house, doing repairs and yardwork and heavy cleaning whenever he was needed for fifteen, no, nearly twenty, years and except when his wife died and he called to say he was taking her body back to Haiti and couldn't come that week to wash the windows, he had never mentioned his family. And I never asked, thinks Hope. Should I have asked? Did they even want me to ask, she wonders. Maybe they would have felt I was intrusive. But I might have been able to help. She cringes remembering that earlier today she has bragged about her children to them, trumpeting all their accomplishments and successes. How thoughtless, she thinks, how cruel. It's bad enough for them that life is so unfair without one of the lucky ones crowing about her blessings.

She creeps back to the sunporch and returns to the kitchen, making a noisy entrance. Paul is still polishing silver. Annie has put the cake in the oven and is seasoning the roast they will have for dinner.

"As soon as you finish that, Annie, you and Paul have some lunch, and then I want you to go upstairs and take a rest on one of the beds in the guest room. This is going to be a long day for you, and I don't want you to wear yourself out before the party begins. Paul, is there any chance you can stay and help Annie tonight?"

Paul thinks a minute before answering. "Well, I can't stay straight through, Miz Waring. I got to pick up my daughter and her children and take her to get her car if it's ready. But I can come back after that, if it would be a help to you."

"Oh, yes, Paul. It would be a great help to me and to Annie too. You can do the drinks and serve dinner. Now you do like I said, Annie, and take a rest, a nap, if you can. I'm going to eat some of your cookies and a glass of milk in the library.

As she is finishing her snack, she hears Annie plodding up the stairs. She goes back to the kitchen where Paul has just completed the silver. "Oh, Paul, it's beautiful. Nobody polishes silver like you." And she leads him into the living room and shows him the draperies and the slipcovers and the portrait of Sam that she wants hung in the library over the mantel. Then she goes back to the kitchen and arranges her flowers.

When Sam comes home from the University, he gives no sign that this important day is different from any other. He is an ascetic man not given to emotions. Hope suspects that she is the only person who knows that beneath his austere exterior there is more warmth than anyone else can imagine and a peculiar sense of humor that he rarely exhibits. Even his children have always been a little afraid of him. He is a dry teacher, no Mr. Chips, she thinks, but there are graduate students who have worked under his direction who she knows regard him as the best in his department.

"Lovely flowers, dear," he says, the nearest thing to a compliment he ever gives, and goes up to change his clothes. She follows him and sees, as he starts to put on an old pair of trousers and a baggy sweater, that he has completely forgotten their party. When she reminds him, he puts back on the suit he was wearing. "They had a party at work for me today too, you know. President Hamill was there. Good cake. Better quality Scotch than usual. Big crowd. Several speeches about how great I am. Embarrassing, but you would have liked it. Why weren't you there?"

"Because nobody, including you, asked me to come," she says. But she says it in a teasing voice and with a smile. "Besides I was getting ready for our party here. All the children are coming."

"Oh, dear," he says. "Two parties in one day. All the children? Not I hope, the grandchildren."

"No," she assures him, "no grandchildren. But they've all written you poems to be read before dinner."

"Good God," he says, and sighs deeply.

She smiles at him. Nothing he has said is to be taken seriously, she knows. It is only the usual banter that passes for conversation between them.

Downstairs again, they wait for the children's arrival. Tom and Mary are the first to arrive. Tom brings a bottle of wine, nothing special, but he has always been close with money, and his new position as partner in a prestigious New York law firm and the large increase in his income do not seem to have changed him. He kisses his mother, hugs his father, and Sara does the same. The Warings are particularly fond of Sara, who tells Hope that she looks beautiful in the new dress she has bought for this occasion. Turning to Sam, she kisses him and says she hopes they will see more of him now that he won't be working all the time. Sam clears his throat and says nothing, but Hope can see he is pleased. For a little while they all talk together of the grandchildren and their activities, and especially of the new baby who already recognizes his sisters and crows with delight when either of them comes in his room.

"I can't say the same," grumbles Tom. "He usually starts crying whenever he sees me."

"Why, honey," says Sara. "That's only because you're working so hard, and he doesn't get to see you as much as he does them. Give him a little time and he'll love you as much as the girls do."

"It wasn't my idea to move to the suburbs," he answers. "Now I'm gone in the morning when he wakes up, and I don't get home till he's in bed."

"I know, I know," says Sara, trying to smooth things over.
But Tom won't let it go.

"If we'd stayed in the city just a few more months until I made partner, we could have afforded to send the children to private schools, and there wouldn't have been any need to move to Chappequa. I spend half my life on that damn train."

Sara is obviously embarrassed by his truculence.

Hope jumps in nervously. She has had plenty of experience in diverting her bulldog son, but before she can say more than "How are the girls liking their new school?" there is the sound of a car in the driveway, and she hastens to the front door. It is Kathy and her husband, but instead of getting out of their car, they sit and talk. When they do come up to the door, Hope can see from Frank's angry face and Kathy's flushed one that they have been quarreling. But they *never* fight, thinks Hope. Oh dear, what can be wrong?

She hugs and kisses them both—she has always liked Frank—and leads them into the living room and calls Paul to fix them drinks. Frank greets everyone with an uncharacteristic lack of enthusiasm and crosses to sit by Sara. Kathy kisses her father and wishes him a happy birthday, kisses her brother, and takes her seat between the two of them. She and Frank stare at each other across the room. It looks as if her children and the in-laws and are facing off as teams.

But Tom breaks ranks. He looks at his wristwatch and rolls his eyes. "Where on earth is Richie?—late as usual? Sara and I have to drive back early, because I have an important breakfast meeting with a client. Richie never thinks of anyone's situation but his own."

"Oh, Tom, do shut up," says Kathy. "You've made partner now, so you don't need to be jealous of Richie's success anymore. Don't spoil Daddy's birthday by one of your stupid quarrels."

He turns toward her angrily. She has cut close to the bone, but Sara—what a dear girl, thinks Hope—rises and crosses to him. She takes his hand and says to him and to the room at large, "Tell them what the head partner said to you, Tom. Now, all of you, listen to this."

"Well," says Tom, and he actually looks embarrassed and proud at the same time. "He told me I'd made partner, and then he said he thought I was the young partner most apt to be appointed to the Court. He meant The Pennsylvania Supreme Court. He said he didn't think he'd live long enough to see it happen, but that he would do everything he could to help me. He said he just missed his own chance in '85, but he'd learned a lot about politics since then and he'd do his best to see I made it."

Hope feels a rush of pride for her son, and Sam rises and makes a toast to him. "To my oldest son, whose hard work and dedication I have long admired, and to the great future, whatever it may be, that I have no doubt lies ahead for him." He catches Tom in a strong embrace, and the two of them sit down with tears in their eyes.

Saved this time by Sara, thinks Hope, but she soon sees Tom eyeing his watch again and fears his temper will once more explode if the others don't come soon. But then there is the sound of a car outside, and in less than ten seconds, Richie bursts into the room pulling his new wife, Ariadne, by her arm.

Not a hello or a happy birthday, just a loud shout to the whole room. "Come out, come right now, you won't be sorry. Come and see my new Lexus!"

There is a large fire in the fireplace, and all of them would prefer to bask in its warmth and ignore his summons. But the force of his will is too strong. They rise and troupe out together into the cold night, and there in the driveway is the car, gleaming silver in the soft light from the front porch.

Sara makes the first move toward it. Still holding Tom's hand, she draws him along with her. "It's beautiful, Richie, just beautiful." Tom is mesmerized by the car. He stares at it as though he has never seen one like it. Perhaps he hasn't, for it really is exceptional. Richie is obviously waiting for him to make some comment, and when he doesn't, he turns with a shrug to the rest of the family. Unfortunately for him, his parents are indifferent to all automobiles; they are just conveyances to take them from one place to another. Sam tries his best to show enthusiasm, but his efforts fall short.

"That's a fine car, Son," he says, but even to him it sounds lame.

What does one say about a car, thinks Hope desperately, understanding just how important it is to Richie that they appreciate his new acquisition, but before she can think of anything, Frank steps into the breach.

"That's some car, fellow," he says, peering into the interior. "My God, just look at these seats—real leather—they even smell good. And you've got that new map system. How does it work?"

"It's great. I used it on the way down here, and it came up with some short cuts that I've never discovered myself."

Frank has more questions, and Hope, seeing that the others are cold, herds them back into the house, leaving the two men outside peering at the car motor.

But before they get inside, Richie calls out to his father, "Hey, Dad, there's a storm coming and I'd like to put the Lexus in your garage."

"I'm afraid my car is already in there for the night," Sam answers.

"Well, that's all right. Just throw me your keys and I'll get it out."

Sam hesitates slightly, then tosses him his keys and joins the others in the house.

Inside Hope turns her attention to her newest daughter-in-law.

"Ariadne, you look even more beautiful than the last time we were together. That was at the Pritchard's party, I think." She feels that she is always trying unsuccessfully to warm up this cool second wife of Richie's, his trophy wife, she thinks. Ariadne is a model, a profession that Hope has discovered requires a great deal of self-discipline. She admires her daughter-in-law for this quality which she has in abundance, but she wishes she were not such an "ice maiden," Kathy's name for her.

"How are the children?—it's been so long since we've seen them." Richie's first wife, Jean, has custody of his two sons. They spend every other weekend with Richie and Ariadne, and Richie makes little effort to bring them together with their grandparents.

"I don't see much of them either," says Ariadne. "Richie usually takes them on outings during the day, and of course, he and I have adult things to do at night. It's important for both of us to be seen at functions around town for professional reasons."

Oh, those poor little boys, thinks Hope, and resolves to invite Jean to come and bring them for a visit the next weekend they are with her.

Frank and Richie make a noisy reappearance, taking animatedly about cam brakes and overdrive. Whatever they are, thinks Hope.

Paul serves another round of drinks, and the party breaks into smaller conversational groups. Kathy has gone to sit with her father and Tom, and they are drawing out their father on the book which will be his first retirement project. Sara—bless her heart—is sitting next to Ariadne and conversing with her more successfully than Hope has ever been able to do. But observing her family Hope feels that something is amiss. Their conversation seems forced, and she feels tension in the room that she cannot identify. Of course Tom and Richie have sparred with each other since they were children, and Ariadne has always seemed stiff and cold to Hope. She probably feels that we regard her as an interloper, she thinks, and Hope admits to herself that she does feel that Ariadne has wrongfully usurped Jean's place, but she always tries hard to overcome these feelings. No, there is something more. Her intuition tells her something is wrong, and she prays that whatever the problem, it won't surface tonight and spoil this special evening for Sam.

In a little while Paul announces dinner. They go to the table and everyone admires the flowers, the shining silver and the pristine linen. They praise Hope for making everything so beautiful, and when the wine is poured, there are toasts to Sam by each of his children. Paul is serving, but when the roast lamb, everyone's favorite, is placed before

Sam for him to carve, there is a call for Annie to present herself for a host of compliments and greetings from the children for whom she was a caretaker for so many years. Perhaps everything is all right after all, thinks Hope, but just as she begins to relax, Richie speaks up.

"I have an announcement, everybody listen up. I know you're all wondering how I came by that swanky car." (It had not occurred to Hope to speculate on how Richie could afford such a car, but it might have, had she known how much it cost.) "Well, this Christmas my bonus was out of the ballpark. I may not be a partner yet, but I'm still two years younger than Tom, so give me a couple more years. Meanwhile Casson, Merwick, and Pershing is now one of the biggest investment firms in New York, and its profits have gone up like a rocket. I happened to bring in a hunk of that money in my accounts, hence the bonus and the car, and also, get this, we've bought a house on St.Criox on a great beach! Feel free to visit."

On the other side of the table and as far down the side as it was possible to place him, Hope sees Tom taking a deep breath and seeming as he did, to grow taller and taller in his chair. This bit of narrative delivered by Richie as he looked directly at Tom was accompanied by a smile that was anything but pleasant. He has thrown down a gauntlet, and Tom is about to respond to the challenge. Hope sees what is happening but feels powerless. Her sons have been rivals all their lives. When they were young, she was able to send them to their rooms, but now.... What did I do to make them so competitive, she wonders, and waits for the storm. But once again Sara is the peacemaker.

She places her hand on Tom's arm, and Hope can see her grip is strong. "Richie, what good news. I am so happy for you." Tom is trying to break in but she refuses to let him. "What a wonderful family of achievers this is! You with your recognition from your firm, Tom making partner at his and being so appreciated by the head partner, and Kathy's award from the Philadelphia Real Estate Association. How lucky we in-laws are to be married to you. I propose a toast to the siblings by their loving spouses."

At that cue she and Ariadne and Frank raise their glasses, as do Hope and Sam, and another crisis is avoided. But was Frank slow to respond to Sara's toast, thinks Hope, almost reluctant? Oh dear, she says to herself, I hope he's not pouting over the quarrel he and Kathy were having when they arrived. It isn't like Frank to pout.

The rest of the meal is eaten in comparative peace, although Hope notices that Richie and Tom are both beginning to look at their watches with increasing frequency. What can be more important than their father's birthday and retirement party, wonders Hope? They are barely pretending to listen to what he is saying. Of course he's telling old stories that they've heard many times before, but that's what families are for, to listen to stories over and over until they become part of the family history. And Sam enjoys the telling so much.

Finally it is dessert time. Paul brings in the cake, coconut, Sam's favorite. Annie comes from the kitchen, and all together, they sing a loud and harmonious Happy Birthday. Sam is immensely pleased and compliments Annie on the cake. When ice cream and strawberries, a Warring birthday tradition, are served, Hope notices that Ariadne looks longingly at them but eats only the strawberries.

Then dinner is over, and Hope rises to lead them into the library where the new portrait of Sam has been hung. It is to be the climax of this family party, followed, she hopes, by congenial conversation in this small, intimate room, where Paul has laid a fire while they were eating. But Richie says as he stands, "Sorry to eat and run, Mom. It's been a great party, but Ariadne and I promised to stop in at the Fanning's tonight, and we'll just make their reception for the mayor."

And before she can protest, Tom says, "We should go now too. I have an early breakfast with a client, and I need to get a decent night's sleep. He's a bear, and I have to be on my toes to deal with him."

Hope tries to keep her disappointment out of her voice. "Of course, I understand, but before you go, I have something special to show you."

She leads them into the den. The two men have picked up their coats, and are struggling into them as they enter the room. The portrait hangs above the mantle. It is a handsome painting, with Sam's strong intellect and a hint of his dry humor clearly defined.

"Oh, Daddy, it's wonderful. It's you, you exactly!" cries Kathy, and the rest echo her sentiments. Everyone has something complimentary to say about it, and Hope can tell their enthusiasm is genuine. She breathes a sigh of relief and satisfaction. At least this moment has gone right.

And then with a whirl of thanks and kisses and goodbyes, her sons and their wives are out the door. Now at least, she thinks, Sam and I can sit and visit with Kathy and Frank.

But before she reaches her chair, Kathy takes her arm and, with a meaningful look at Frank, pulls her out to the sun porch. The door to the kitchen is cracked, and Hope can hear Annie and Paul quietly cleaning up from the party. The sun porch is unheated and there is only a little light, but Hope can see that she is not going to like what Kathy has brought her here to say. Something about her face looks so vulnerable, and she is having trouble finding words. She seems almost paralyzed.

"What is it, dear? What do you want to say? Is it the children?. Are they all right? Yes, of course they are or you wouldn't be here. So what can it be? Are you ill? Is Frank?"

Kathy finally begins to speak. "No, nothing like that. Oh, Mother, I really didn't want to tell you tonight. The others know, and I've been afraid all night that one of them would slip and say something. You might hear it from anyone though—we haven't been able to keep it much of a secret. So I think I have to tell you myself before you hear it from somebody else. I'm so sorry—I feel like I'm throwing a hand grenade into your life and Dad's."

Hope wants to run back to the den, away from what Kathy is about to say. She stares at her daughter, and now she is the one who is speechless.

"Mom, the thing is, Frank and I are getting a divorce."

"No, Kathy, no, that can't be. You've always been so happy together, and Frank adores you. And the children, you're both such good parents. You can't hurt them this way. Whatever Frank has done, you can forgive him, I know. Just forgive him, Kathy, and it will be all right."

Kathy took a deep breath. "Mom, it isn't Frank, it's me. I want this divorce for me. I can't stay in this marriage any longer."

"Oh, Kathy, you don't mean that. You love Frank, I know you do. Whatever the problems are, you and Frank can work them out if you try."

"But I don't want to try, Mom. I haven't been happy with Frank for a long time. He's lost all of whatever ambition he ever had. He's just marking time at this computer job. Almost every night he leaves dinner to play with that crazy rock band—there's no money in that. Then on weekends, when I have to work with clients—I'm the one who makes the real money—instead of taking care of the kids, he lies on the sofa and watches sports games. I feel like I'm doing all the heavy lifting in this marriage. I don't love Frank anymore. I want a different kind of marriage."

"I can't bear it. This isn't you, Kathy, hurting so many people so you can have what you want. You've always bulldozed people to have your way, but this is too much. Are you really my child? I feel as though a space alien has taken over your body."

"I'm sorry, Mom. I'm trying to be honest with you. I've done my best to make this marriage work, and I've tried to make it look good from the outside. You can't know the inside of anyone else's marriage, not even your child's.

"I have to go now. We can talk another time, but you need to know that nothing you say is going to change my mind." She gives her mother's unyielding body a brief hug, then goes to the den to say goodbye to her father.

Hope feels sick with grief. She slips onto the back porch and sinks into a chair in the corner. In a few minutes she hears Frank and Kathy's car pulling out of the driveway.

In the darkness she begins to cry. She sheds tears of grief and anger and pity for her grandchildren and for Frank and, yes, for herself and Sam. She has been through the divorce of Richie and Jean, and she knows how much pain and ugliness can be involved. The rejection by a much loved partner engenders hatred and vindictiveness that is unimaginable at the beginning of the divorce process. She had been sick at heart when Richie's affair with Ariadne ended his marriage with Jean. Richie vowed to Hope that he would be fair and generous, but he became vindictive when Jean sought more support than he was willing to give her. It had been a nightmare. How can Kathy leave Frank when she has seen in her own family how much grief and pain divorce causes?

The kitchen door to the porch opens. Annie and Paul are leaving. Hope scrunches down in her chair so that they won't see her sitting here in the cold. But she can hear their voices.

"Poor Miz Waring," says Annie. "She and Professor Waring are nice people, and they don't deserve the children they got. I've known Tom and Richie since they was little, and they was always fighting and wanting what the other had. They're still at it now they're grown. Miz Waring couldn't deal with them when they were little, and she sure can't now. Seems like they've always overwhelmed her. And the Professor wasn't much help, always buried in his books. And Kathy—I've known her since she was born. A pretty little girl and could be real sweet, but don't get in the way when there's something she wants. She'll just run right over you."

"You think Frank gonna give her a hard time?" asked Paul.

Hope realizes they have overheard what she and Kathy have been saying.

"I don't think he's planning on it now—he's a pretty nice guy, that Frank, but I expect he will later on, yeah, I reckon he will. You could tell Miz Waring is all broke up about her kids getting divorces, but times has changed. Now people just want what they think is gonna make *them* happy. They think you shouldn't have to work to make things right. Her kids has made a lot of money, but they're selfish people. But she ain't the only one whose kids have gone wrong."

Their voices are fading as they walk out to Paul's car behind the house.

Hope remains cold and miserable in the porch chair. She feels sure that Frank has told Sam about the divorce while she was with Kathy. She will have to go in to him soon, and they will comfort each other, but she stills needs a little time alone now to mourn what is lost. She can never feel the same again about her family that she loves so much. It was bad enough when Richie and Jean's marriage failed, but this is Kathy, her youngest, her only daughter, her baby girl, who is about to cause great pain to her children and Frank. All I wanted for all of them was a marriage like Sam's and mine, loving and forgiving, she thinks. How unfair, how cruel life can be.

She knows Sam is in the library waiting for her, and so she dries her eyes and goes in to him. Kathy has always been his pet, and she knows that he is as sick at heart as she is. He is sitting with his head in his hands, and she sits beside him on the sofa, and they put their arms around each other. There is nothing to say for comfort, only the silent holding, and the hands that slide up and down each other's backs. Something is broken that will never be mended, she thinks. Nothing will ever be the same. But when Sam pulls back and looks into her face and says, "Together we'll weather this somehow, Hope," despite all her doubts, she answers, "Yes, yes, we will."

# A Butterfly for my Cocoon

On a Wednesday in early November, Alice Carrington took a train from Bronxville into Manhattan for an early afternoon appointment with her dentist. But when she reached his office, she found he had been taken ill and was gone for the day.

"So sorry, Mrs. Carrrington," said his receptionist. "I tried to call you, but you had already left."

Alice stood on the curb in front of his office building, trying to decide what to do with this unexpected gift of time. Should she go to Saks and get an early start on her Christmas shopping? Or perhaps she should just take a train home and treat herself to an afternoon with the new book she had bought the day before. In the end she decided to walk across town to her daughter's apartment. The walk would be good for her, and if Sarah wasn't there, she would take a cab to Grand Central and the train home.

As she crossed a street in a residential neighborhood of fine townhouses, she saw about halfway down the block a pile of some kind of debris on the curb. A young couple were pulling objects out of it, and as she got closer, she saw that they were salvaging a small table and two chairs. They were laughing and exclaiming as they rooted through the pile, but by the time she reached it, they were struggling awkwardly down the sidewalk with their loot.

Alice stopped to look at the mound of someone's once cherished possessions. Why are they here, she wondered? Are these the remnants of someone's life, unwanted by her heirs? Or is this the detritus of a divorce? Or has someone moved to a splendid new home and left these bits and pieces behind as unworthy of a grander setting?

Then she saw the baby buggy. It had slipped off the pile into the gutter where it must have been hit by a car. One side was caved in and the undercarriage was badly mangled. A wheel was lying some ten feet away, crushed almost beyond recognition. But the buggy was made of wicker and Alice saw its charm. It must be seventy-five, maybe a hundred years old, she thought. My mother could have been pushed in a buggy like that. Oh, I must have it—Sarah will love it for her baby, I know. It will have to be mended, of course, but I can get that done before the baby comes." She hailed a cab and persuaded the driver to load the buggy and wheel into his trunk for the short drive to Sarah's apartment. The doorman carried it into the lobby for her, and she called Sarah on the intercom to come down and see a "surprise."

"She's going to love it when she sees it," she told the doorman.

But Sarah didn't love it.

"Mother, are you out of your mind? A piece of trash out of a junk pile! I can't believe you picked this thing up out of the gutter and brought it to my apartment. What were you thinking?"

"Sarah, it's an antique. Nobody makes buggies out of wicker any more. If I went out to look for a buggy like this, I probably couldn't find one in a million years. They were made by hand—look at the way these edges are woven together. It's beautiful work."

"Mother, it's road kill and it's filthy. You'll never get it clean, and it's broken beyond repair. And what would you ever do with it anyway?"

"Why, Sarah, it's for you, you and the baby. I know it's broken and dirty now, but I can get it cleaned and repaired before the baby comes and, trust me, it will be beautiful."

Sarah began to realize that the buggy meant something to her mother beyond being an antique or an object of fine craftsmanship and she softened her tone.

"Mom, I know if you say so, it can be made into something beautiful, but I don't need it. The fact is, Bobby's mother has offered us the carriage she used for him. It's one of those English ones that you see being pushed through parks in London by nurses and nannies—very much the in thing right now. It's the Rolls Royce of buggies. Bobby and I could never afford one on our own, so it's a great offer from Mrs. Randolph."

"Yes," said Alice. "Of course I can understand why you would want to use it, especially if it was Bobby's when he was a baby." And she did understand, but then out of the blue, one of those cursed hot flashes rolled over her, and she felt very tired and ready to go home. "I should really be thinking about getting myself to Grand Central. I don't want to get caught in that rush hour crowd."

Sarah tried to persuade her that it was too early for rush hour and urged her to come upstairs for a cup of tea and some good talk, but Alice was adamant. There was a place in her heart where it felt as if anger and hurt had been squeezed into a hard little knot, and she didn't want Sarah to know she was capable of such pettiness.

"No, no, I really can't stay now. I'll drive in to pick up the buggy tomorrow and have lunch with you then if you like. Wallace, could you get me a cab, please? And could you lock that buggy in some closet in the basement. I promise you I'll take it home in my car tomorrow."

Alice slept poorly that night. She spent her wakeful moments telling herself that Sarah had a perfect right to her own preference, that it was important that she nurture her relationship with her rather difficult mother-in-law by accepting the English buggy, and that the wicker buggy might be too fragile for New York anyway. By morning the little knot of bitterness she had been harboring was mostly gone, and she was in a cheerful mood when she arrived at Sarah's apartment.

Sarah had made an especially nice lunch for her (a small act of expiation perhaps, thought Alice.) They spoke of family matters, and Sarah talked about her pregnancy symptoms. Alice promised that she and Sarah's father would postpone their annual stay in the Berkshires until August, so that she could be on hand when the baby arrived in late June.

"Thanks, Mom," said Sarah. "I do appreciate your willingness to be here, but Mrs. Randolph has already hired some famous New York baby nurse to come in and help me when I come home from the hospital. You and Dad go ahead and take your vacation just as you always do."

"Well, yes, if that's what you want, dear." But it's not what I wanted, she thought.

Up until then they had both avoided speaking of the buggy, but now Sarah brought it up. "You know, if you wanted to, you could offer that wicker buggy to Chrissie. She might really go for it."

Alice was puzzled. "Is there something I don't know?"

"Oh dear, I guess I've put my foot in my mouth again. I know she's planning to tell you and Dad she's pregnant when you have dinner with them on Thanksgiving, but I forgot. Please don't let her know I said anything. I'm sure she and Thomas want to tell you themselves."

"When is her baby due? The same time as yours, I suppose?" asked Alice. "They'll be almost like twins."

"Well, not exactly. "She's three months ahead of me. She's due in April."

"Oh, I see," said Alice. She tried as hard as she could to keep her tone neutral, to avoid that plaintive note that she hated in other's voices and even more in her own. She had worked hard to have a good relationship with her daughter-in-law, whom she really liked. But why are we always the last to know anything important in their lives, she wondered? At least Thomas could have told us. After all he has lunch with his dad in New York once or twice a week. She felt that knot in her stomach begin to grow again.

The next morning she drove to Ossining to Kowski's Furniture Repair and Refinishing Shop. When she entered it, she looked around nervously for Mr. Kowski and, yes, he was still there, still alive, although he must be well into his eighties by now. And he recognized her!

"Mrs. Carrington!" he said in his funny accented English. "Are you bringing me more of that beautiful wicker from your mother's house? What can I do for you today?"

She took him out to the street to show him the buggy and watched him anxiously as he examined it.

"Well," he said finally, "it's a shame it's so smashed up, a beautiful piece of workmanship like that. But I think I can fix it so you can use it if you want to. It's just that the natural wicker has darkened with age quite a lot, so any repairs will really show, unless you're willing to have it painted."

"I would love to have it painted," said Alice. "Cream color, I think. The same color you used for my mother's wicker, that soft cream. Then those interesting little designs around the edges and on the sides could be touched up in pastels. I think I could do that myself.

"But what about the undercarriage and the wheel, Mr. Kowski?" she added.

"There's a welder at the garage at the foot of the street who can probably fix the undercarriage and find you a wheel. His name is Lobo—tell him I sent you. I'll take the buggy apart, and you can take the undercarriage to him right now. And believe me, it will be worth whatever you have to pay to get this buggy in good shape again—it's a beauty. And you found it in a gutter in New York? Well, I always said you had an eye, Mrs. Carrington."

Alice felt like kissing Mr. Kowski.

"What a nice compliment. It really means something coming from a true master craftsman. I was beginning to doubt my own judgment."

And she was off down the street to the garage where she left the undercarriage and wheels with Lobo and drove away with her confidence restored. Yes, she thought, it will be a prize when it's done. I was right to pick it out of the gutter.

On Thanksgiving when she and her husband arrived at the little caretaker's house that her son and his wife rented on an estate in Bedford, she saw a Mercedes parked behind Tom's car.

"Oh, damn, that woman is here!" she said aloud, and immediately wished she hadn't.

"What woman, Ally?" asked Roger.

"Chrissie's mother, Mrs. Cane. We haven't seen Thomas and Chrissie in weeks, and I was hoping for a nice visit with them. That woman is such a pain. Talks all the time, won't let anyone else get in a word, wants to run everything. She's the reason they're in this house. She wanted them here in Bedford where she can drop in on Chrissie all the time. Oh, I wish we didn't have to be with her today."

But there was nothing they could do but force smiles and enter the house. Chrissie greeted them, and it was obvious even to Roger who was usually oblivious to such matters that she was pregnant.

"Goodness," he said. "What a surprise! Well, congratulations to both of you." And he kissed his daughter-in-law and hugged his son.

"Chrissie, we're thrilled," said Alice, and she, too, kissed Chrissie and would have embraced Thomas except that Mrs. Cane was suddenly between them, an arm around each of the young people, drawing them close to her and beaming her wide smile at the Carringtons.

"Isn't it exciting?" she said. "I guessed, of course, when Chrissie was so sick last summer. Mothers have a way of sensing these things, don't they, Alice?"

"You've known since last summer?" asked Alice weakly.

"I had a lot of trouble in those first months, Alice," said Chrissie. "My doctor was afraid I might lose the baby, so I didn't want to get everyone's hopes up. But now he says everything is all right, so today is a celebration. Also we know now it's a girl, so we're celebrating that, too."

"A girl!" exclaimed Mrs. Cane. "How wonderful. Oh, Chrissie, your father would have been so happy. He always favored little girls. My angel, he called you. He would have made the perfect grandfather."

There was an awkward pause before they went into the living room. Alice saw that it was strewn with tissue and ribbon and baby toys and clothing.

"Since we're celebrating, I brought a few things for my grandchild-to-be. Let me show you, Alice. There are such adorable things for babies these days," said Mrs. Cane.

Chrissie looked quickly at Alice.

"Mother, we can do that later," she said. She gathered up everything she could carry and took it all back to her bed room. "Now I want you to help me with dinner. I can't tell if this turkey is done or not, and I need you to make the gravy." She whisked her mother into the kitchen with her.

The rest of the day went about the same. When the Carringtons left, Thomas walked out to the car with them.

"I'm sorry about all that," he said. "It's hard for Chrissie, too. She's sorry for her mother because she's all alone now, but she sees that she's difficult. She knows you would rather be here when her mother isn't, but Thanksgiving and all, you know, being an only child, well, she feels obligated. Mom, why don't you come into New York one day and have lunch with Dad and me? Maybe Sarah would come too."

"That would be lovely, dear," said Alice, brightening at the thought of a luncheon (what would you say, she wondered, *a quartre?*) with her children and Roger.

He hugged them both, and Alice held him a little longer. So young for all these responsibilities, she thought, only twenty-three. But I was only twenty-two when I married, and I was pregnant with Sarah when I was twenty-three. Why does it all seem so different now? Why was I so eager to have grandchildren, and now that both my children are about to have children of their own, why doesn't it seem so wonderful? Am I envious of my children? No, of course not. It must be because having grandchildren means getting old, and I'm not ready for that yet—hairs on my chin and flabby arms and all that. "Past my prime." Oh, what I wouldn't give to be back in my prime.

"Well, how do you like it, Mrs. Carrington. Is the color what you wanted? Do the wheels look too new? Do you think they're the right size?"

"It's perfect, Mr. Kowski, just perfect. But I always knew it would be. I always had faith in your ability to bring it back to life."

"Now may I ask you what you are going to do with it?"

"I'm not sure yet. You see, both my daughter and daughter-in-law are expecting."

"And they both will want it, and you don't know which one to give such a prize to. I can see that's a very hard dilemma."

Alice didn't try to explain any further. She didn't want to say that Sarah didn't want the buggy, and that whether Chrissie wanted it or not, she wasn't sure she wanted to give it to her.

When she got home again, she rolled the buggy through the house and out to the sunroom. Oh, it's perfect here, she thought, a kind of decorative piece to go with Mother's wicker furniture. In the next few days she used acrylic paints in pink, blue and green to highlight the decorative designs in the wicker. She worked to have it finished by Christmas when both of her children and their spouses were coming for the day, and she made her deadline, but then decided she didn't want to show it to them until the lining was done and hid it in the garage under a sheet.

Christmas was a happy family day. There was much conversation about the expected babies, and the furniture, clothing and other equipment their parents were accumulating for them.

"Are you getting playpens?" said Alice. "I don't know how I could have got along without one."

"I don't think most people use those much anymore, Mom," said Sarah. "Too confining."

"But that's just the point, dear," said Alice. "Babies need to be confined so they won't hurt themselves."

"I have a good friend who tried to use one, Alice, but she says her baby screamed every time she put him in it," said Chrissie. "She said it just wasn't worth it."

Alice started to say that babies had to be put in playpens early so they would get used to them, but she saw that her children weren't interested in her opinions. I was a good mother, she thought. I had happy babies and I loved taking care of them. And now all I learned from those years of experience doesn't mean a thing. Nobody cares. Why do those years, the good years when you can have children and take care of them, go by so fast? Why didn't I have more when I could? I should have argued more when Roger thought two were enough. When I knew I was menopausal, I thought, well, now I can't have any more babies, but I can be a grandmother—but that doesn't seem very rewarding so far. She felt the knot twist in her stomach again.

In early January, she took the buggy to her upholsterer to have a lining made for it. She had found a plastic covered bassinet mattress that only needed a little alteration to fit the buggy, and she had a piece of silk she wanted quilted to line the sides and cover the mattress. Mr. Grover showed her how he could use Velcro to make the lining removable. "Yes," she said, when he draped the fabric to show her how it would look, "that's just perfect, Mr. Grover, just the way I envisioned it."

It was ready for her to pick up in just two weeks. She rolled it back into the sunroom and regarded it with admiration. I did it, she thought. I brought it back to life. It's probably even lovelier now than it was when it was new.

It was in the sunroom when Chrissie stopped by for an unexpected visit. She went straight out to sit on one of the chaises where she could put her feet up but stopped in from of the buggy.

"Oh, Alice, how beautiful! Where on earth did you find it? It must be for Sarah's baby. She'll love it."

"I don't know, Chrissie. It's not very practical, I guess. Not good for New York's dirty sidewalks and no better for where you are, out in the country with no sidewalks at all. More for show than anything else, I guess. Actually I like the way it looks just on display here with all the other wicker."

"You're right, it's perfect for this room. Well, maybe your grandbabies can sleep in it here sometime. Lucky babies. It's fit for a princess."

Chrissie sighed a deep sigh, and Alice saw that she coveted the buggy and would take it in a minute, sidewalks or no sidewalks, if it were offered. She almost said, "Take it, it's my present for my first grandchild," but something held her back. I don't want to give it up, she thought, even to someone who admires it as much as I do. I want it myself.

At the end of the month, there was one of those winter anomalies, a cloudless day with the temperature hitting the sixties at noon. Alice decided to take the buggy out and push it around the block. A test run, she said to herself. And it rolled along as smoothly as she had imagined it would. It only needs a baby to make it complete, she thought.

At home whenever she sat in the sunroom to read, she found herself pulling the buggy to the side of her chaise where she could hold on to the handle. Unconsciously she pushed it back and forth, and sometimes she hummed the lullabies she used to sing to her children when they were small. She was careful not to do these things when Roger was there. He wouldn't understand, she thought.

She pushed the buggy outside on the rare days when the sun was shining. One day she got as far as the village, and passing in front of "Sumptuous Toys," she saw in the window an array of dolls. One caught her eye immediately. It was life size and had dark curly hair and fat pink cheeks. Just like Sarah and Thomas, she thought, and went right into the store and bought it. She tucked it into the buggy and rolled it home. Yes, this buggy did need a baby, she said to herself, and she does look so sweet in there all covered up with that little pink coverlet. "Anne Marie," she said out loud, "that's your name because I always wanted to name a little girl Anne Marie, but when Roger's mother died just before Sarah was born, well, what could I do but name her Sarah? But now you'll be my Anne Marie."

When she got home, she went up to the attic and got out all Sarah's baby dresses and washed and ironed them. They were so dear with their puffed sleeves and smocking. "These are going to Chrissie for her little girl," she told Anne Marie as she dressed her in a pink dress embroidered with flowers, "but for now you can wear them. Oh, you do look so adorable!"

It took Roger a week to notice the doll in the buggy. He had never been a very observant man. "What's this doll in your buggy, Ally?" he called to her in the kitchen.

"That's a present for Chrissie's little girl when she's old enough for it," she called back. "Doesn't she look like Sarah and Thomas when they were babies?"

"Looks like a doll to me," said Roger, sitting down to have his drink and read the paper.

Cold weather returned, and there were only a few days when Alice could take Anne Marie outside. When it was warm enough, she sometimes went to a small neighborhood park two blocks away where she sat on a bench while Anne Marie slept. One day a young woman with a toddler asleep in a stroller sat down beside her.

"What an extraordinary buggy!" she exclaimed. "I've never seen anything like it. It must be an antique, but it's in such perfect condition. Someone really went to a lot of trouble to get it looking like that."

"Yes. Yes, I did. I wanted it for a gift for a special baby, my godchild, in fact," said Alice, hearing herself and scarcely knowing where the words were coming from. "You see, her mother is very young and inexperienced and needs a great deal of help from me. I've had a wealth of experience with babies, so of course she relies on me for advice. I often take care of Anne Marie. She's a very good baby, sleeps almost all the time."

"Lucky for you," said the young woman. "The only way I can get Peter to sleep in the daytime is to push him in his stroller."

At home Alice rehearsed her conversation in the park. Why on earth did I lie like that, she wondered. I've never made up stories like that in my life. It must be all those hormones Dr. Fowlkes has me on.

In early March, Alice had a call from her best friend, Patty Brewer. "Oh, Alice," she cried. "You'll never guess! Lily is pregnant, due in October. We're going to be grandmothers at almost the same time. Isn't that wonderful? I'm going down to Atlanta when the baby is born. Lily begged me to come. She said, 'Mom, I'm scared to death. I don't know a thing about taking care of a baby, and you've always been so good with them. You'll have to come and stay until I can manage on my own.' And so I have to go, of course."

"Of course," said Alice.

"Oh, you're so lucky. Both of yours will be near enough for you to see them all the time. Atlanta is so far away. But Lily will bring the baby for visits, and you and I can get them together for play times just like we did with our own children. We'll be grandmothers together, Alice. Chrissie's baby is due next month, isn't she? You must be so excited!"

"Of course," said Alice again. Patty paused a minute and changed the subject.

After that conversation, Alice avoided calling Patty. I'll make it up to her later, she thought. It's just too hard to talk to her right now. She also found it hard to leave Anne Marie alone in the house. I know it's irrational, she thought. What could possibly happen to her? Well, the house could burn down, she told herself and shuddered. She began to make excuses to avoid going out at night with Roger.

"Why did you do that?" he asked when he overheard her turn down an invitation to a cocktail party. "You like the Moores, and you've always loved their parties."

"Just not up to it right now, Roger," she replied, and was grateful that he didn't question her further.

Sometimes in the afternoons she sat in the wicker rocking chair on the sunporch and rocked Anne Marie and sang to her. She talked to her too, as she had to Sarah and Thomas, and recited nursery rhymes. "This was Thomas' favorite, Anne Marie. You'll like it too, I know. 'Hickory, dickory, dock...'" I know what I'm doing is a little strange, she thought, but I can't see any harm, and I do enjoy it.

In early March, Chrissie had her baby. Alice and Roger went the next day to see their new grandchild and to take flowers to Chrissie. Thomas wasn't there, and Chrissie's mother was hovering over her daughter's hospital bed.

"Oh, what a shame," she said. "Chrissie just nursed the baby, and they've taken her back to the nursery. But you can go look at her through the glass. She's the dearest little baby in the world. Looks just like Chrissie did when she was born. You'll adore her!"

Alice and Roger went dutifully to the nursery, and a nurse held up the baby for them to admire. She lay in the nurse's arms, fast asleep, a fair and delicate child.

"Mrs. Cane must be right," said Alice. "She certainly isn't like our babies with their dark hair and little chipmunk cheeks."

"Chrissie is blonde and petite," said Roger. "It isn't surprising that her baby would be the same."

"I know, I know," said Alice. She couldn't think of any way to explain that the child somehow seemed alien to her without sounding unnatural.

Back in Chrissie's room they sang the baby's praises. Then—"A perfect angel. Have you named her yet?" asked Alice.

"We thought, Ellen Leigh," said Chrissie.

"What a lovely name," said Alice, relieved that it wasn't Ida, after Mrs. Cane. She particularly disliked that name. But did I dislike it before I knew her, or just since, she wondered?

"They wanted to name her after me, of course," said Mrs. Cane. "'First daughter after the mother's mother,' you know. But I already have a niece named for me, and so I told them I'd be just as happy to have her named after my mother."

"I have a silver cup that belonged to Thomas that I want Ellen Leigh to have," Alice said to Chrissie. "I just want to get her name engraved on the other side of it. He drank out of that cup for years, Chrissie. I think you'll like it."

"Oh my, Alice," said Mrs. Cane before Chrissie could speak. "The young don't want to be bothered with silver polishing these days. Pewter is nice and doesn't need all that cleaning."

"Mother!" said Chrissie. She turned to Alice. "Of course I'd love Thomas' cup for Ellen. What a lovely thing for her to have with all those associations with her father. It will be a pleasure to polish it."

On the drive home, Alice said to Roger, "I didn't think Chrissie had it in her to put her mother in her place. Maybe I've underestimated her."

On her first visit to Chrissie after she came home from the hospital, Alice was dismayed to see the Mercedes in the drive. She groaned and considered driving off and trying again later, but too late, there was Mrs. Cane at the door.

"How nice to see you," she called. "Oh, thank you, I'll put this delicious smelling casserole in the kitchen, and they can have it for dinner tonight. Chrissie will be so pleased—she still isn't doing much cooking yet. I've been helping out as much as I can, but tonight I'm invited to a party in Katonah that I don't want to miss. The baby just went to sleep and won't be awake for awhile, but Chrissie is in her room, and I know she wants to see you, so why don't you go back there and visit with her?"

She's trying to be nice, thought Alice. I wonder what happened. I think Chrissie must have said something to her—I can't imagine what—but it seems to be working. Or could it be that Ellen—she's her first grandchild too—has put a charm on her?

When she went into Chrissie's room, she found her fast asleep and crept out without waking her. "She needs her sleep, Ida. I'll come back another day." But before she could go, Mrs. Cane took her arm and drew her into the baby's room to the crib.

"I know you'll want to see Ellen," she whispered. "Look, isn't she dear?"

Alice looked down at the little head. She gently reached down to place her hand on the downy blond fuzz—so soft, she thought. She watched the pulses beating in the baby's temples, felt through her hand on Ellen's back the throbbing of her heart. I've never seen her eyes or heard her make a sound, and yet she's so alive, thought Alice, a tiny living creature. A week ago she didn't exist and now she's here, my grandchild—and yes, Ida Cane's, too, a link between us that exists whether I want it or not.

"Isn't she beautiful?" said Mrs. Cane. "I've been so lonely since Tom died, but now I feel I have something—someone—special to live for."

Alice looked at Ida Cane's face. She was bending over the crib, and her face as she looked at Ellen was suffused with tenderness.

Just then the baby began to stir. She stretched her arms and arched her back. "Oh dear, I've waked her," said Alice.

"Would you like to hold her? It's lovely to hold her," said Mrs. Cane. "Here." And she lifted Ellen out of the crib and put her in Alice's arms.

The baby's head nestled into Alice's neck, and Alice rubbed her cheek over the down on her head, and smelled that never forgotten baby smell, that combination of powder and oil and sour milk and ammonia. Alice closed her eyes and breathed it in. She held Ellen firmly in her arms and turned from side to side, rocking her, listening to her making sucking sounds on her neck. Then she handed her to Mrs. Cane. "You're right, Ida," she said. "It is lovely to hold her. Now, it's your turn. I really must go—I have something to do at home, but I'll be back soon."

In Bronxville there was a message from Sarah on her answering machine. She had had an ultrasound and the baby was fine, and he was a boy.

A boy! First a girl, and now a little boy who will grow and learn to walk and talk and call my name. And I'll be there to see him becoming whoever he will be. Ellen, and now this other one—what a richness of grandchildren, what a future ahead for me, Alice, their grandmother.

She went out to the sunroom and took Anne Marie out of the buggy. She held her as she had held Ellen and turned to rock her in the same way. In her arms the doll was still and lifeless, her latex skin was cold. Alice brushed her cheek across the dark acrylic hair and felt its stiffness. "Don't you mind, Anne Marie," she whispered to the doll, "Don't you mind. Just be patient, and in a year or two, there is a little girl who will love you very much. I promise." The doll stared at her with its blue glass eyes as she carried it upstairs and wrapped it in tissue and put it in a trunk in the attic.

When she came down, she brought a sheet with her and rolled the buggy out to the garage and filled it with the baby dresses she had washed and ironed. Tomorrow, she said to herself, I'll drive to Bedford and give it to Chrissie. She appreciated how special it was as soon as she saw it, just as I did. She said it was fit for a princess, and now she has her own little princess to sleep in it.

Alice looked into the buggy and imagined blond baby Ellen sleeping under the pink coverlet in the nest of quilted silk that she, Alice, had chosen. How perfectly the pale colors, the delicate silk, would suit her. I had a vision for this buggy, she thought, but it was incomplete, a cocoon without a butterfly, but now there's Ellen to be my butterfly. And she smoothed the sheet around the buggy and lifted it into the trunk of the car and gently closed the latch.

978-0-595-37378-9
0-595-37378-X

Printed in the United States
41042LVS00005B/283-378